Mistletoe @ Christmas Tree Lodge

A SECOND CHANCE ROMANCE

JAN JOHNSON

FARMHOUSE
PUBLISHING

Also by Jan Johnson

Mercy Series

My Heart's for You

Windows of My Heart

The Way to My Heart

Memoir

I Will Enter His Gates,

A Walk with God

Books available in audio, print, and ebook

From the first few paragraphs, the writer's style drew me into this romantic holiday tale. I couldn't put it down. The details describing the lodge, the personality of the main character and the fizzled romance were delicious. The author also led you along, each chapter ending with "will they, or won't they get together again?"

I highly recommend picking up this book for a romantic escape.

A charming read. Little Darby was the perfect joy to draw two people back together again over the holidays.

I found myself laughing at the familiar offhanded inner dialogue.

Chapter One

Sophie took in the large stone fireplace and cozy fire licking the logs. A mistletoe ball hung at just the right spot in front of it, strategically placed for great photo ops. A young couple sat at a table with a puzzle and grandparents cuddled with a grandchild reading . The smell of cinnamon filled the room and a table of beautifully iced sugar cookies stood on a plate. And the lobby Christmas tree. It stood clear to the open-beamed ceiling, covered with lights, ribbons, sparkling balls. She swallowed the ache that crept to her throat. This was where Sam had proposed to her. On one knee. In front of a whole room of people. She swallowed. She had to get out of here.

She gathered her long red hair and twisted it into a knot before she sat down in her car. Nothing more annoying than having your hair get entangled in the seat belt. She should just cut it. Nobody needs hair down to their waist. Then again, as much as she hated to admit, it made her stand out, and she enjoyed the frequent compliments.

She pulled out of Christmas Tree Lodge, passing two more

elaborately decorated trees, and onto the two-lane highway headed towards town. Her thoughts were swirling—full of ideas and activities to do with the kiddos staying at the lodge for Christmas. Although she was happily employed substitute teaching second grade, filling in for a teacher on maternity leave, working with kids is what she was made for. She should have the guests do a gingerbread house contest. She smiled.

Maybe having the airline strike which canceled her trip to Europe was something to be grateful for. An opportunity. Who knew what the next week would hold?

Sophie's fingers absent-mindedly wrapped around the sapphire and slid it back and forth on its gold chain. Sam had given it to her the week before he had proposed. She had thought of giving it away, but it was such a beautiful necklace. Sophie turned on the windshield wipers to catch the gentle snowflakes. Sam was now a distant memory. Mostly. Not to say she hadn't been sweating bullets thinking of taking a job at Christmas Tree Lodge. But there was no chance Sam would be there. Right?

She asked Siri to play Christmas music and hummed along —Now the weather outside is frightful...

Sophie drove into the parking lot of the country department store. She got out of the car and tugged her scarf tighter around her neck. Brrr. The temperature was definitely dropping. Snowflakes fell on the Santa hat, covering a carved bear's head. She remembered watched a guy create one, skillfully using his chainsaw on the raw log to turn it into a fun creation. The bell tinkled as she entered. She stopped, stomped her boots, and flicked the snowflakes off her coat.

Now where were the art supplies? She needed glue, construction paper, glitter. What's a project without glitter? Popsicle sticks for ornaments. And string. She loaded her cart and headed to the grocery aisle, looking for graham crackers to build gingerbread houses. Powdered sugar. Candy. Lots of candy.

Her phone buzzed, and she reached into her pocket to answer.

"Oh hey, Claire. Yeah, I know. I wish we could have gone to Europe too. But remember what Grandma always says—there are no problems, only opportunities." Sophie laughed. "Yes, I'm absolutely going to love this job. It's going to be so much fun! Listen, sis, I've got to let you go. I'm at the store." She hung up and smiled.

She wheeled her cart, close to overflowing, to the checkout. The clerk, who couldn't be more than sixteen judging by the attempt to grow facial scruff, let his eyes fall on Sophie's hair. She self-consciously ran her fingers through it. He cleared his throat and continued checking.

"Do you usually get a lot of snow this time of year?" Sophie placed some candy canes on the conveyor belt.

"Sometimes. But I just heard on the news that there's going to be eight inches by midnight. You better get a move on. You don't live around here, do you?" He placed the items into her shopping bag.

"No, just working at the lodge for Christmas."

He handed her the receipt.

"Sounds fun. Don't know if you're interested, but there's always a winter dance there on the twenty-fourth." He held her gaze. "I mean, if there's anyone you'd like to go with."

"I'll keep that in mind." Sophie gave him a smile and headed out, her arms bulging with bags. Memories of that dance, Sam's arms wrapped around her, her head on his chest, moving slowly to the rhythm of I'll Be Home for Christmas, breathing in the scent of his aftershave, listening to the beat of his heart... STOP! She could not let herself go there.

Sophie loaded up all her purchases and started the car,

cranking up the defrost and rubbing her hands together, waiting for the heater to kick in. She should have started out earlier. It was only four, but the sun was just slipping behind Mt. Hood.

The snow covered the roads now, and she was glad to have taken her dad's advice and put on snow tires. She set the heater on seventy-five and let it blow, warming her reddened cheeks.

One week of activities. This was going to be fun. She'd focus on what she did best—working with kids. She loved teaching. Ever since she was small, she would line up her dolls and play school. And when she was in high school, she would volunteer to tutor at the grade school. There had always been a list of teachers begging for her help.

Not knowing if she'd be hired for a permanent position at the school, she applied for her dream job—teaching in an international school. She kept her fingers crossed that this would come to fruition. Might say a few prayers in between.

The lodge came into view. Thousands of white lights twinkled, accentuated by the falling snow. Strings of icicle lights bordered the rafters, a life-sized creche was set up and illuminated, with even a real donkey in the stable.

Sophie parked in the drive through and popped the trunk. It had barely closed with all of her purchases. She started to unload her bags.

"Daddy! You need to help that lady."

She smiled. It was nice to have someone offer to help. A tall shadow rose over her.

"Here, let me help you with those."

That deep voice, though. She swept her hair behind her shoulder with the back of her hand and handed a bag to outstretched arms.

"Daddy, I can get that!"

Sophie reached for another bag and held it out. She drew in a sharp breath as she caught those too familiar hazel eyes.

Sam. What is *he* doing here? And who was that little girl calling him daddy?

Chapter Two

What the heck is Sophie doing here? There was a chance the size of a gnat that she would be here. And yet, here she was.

"Um. Where would you like me to take these?"

Sophie exhaled loudly and placed her hand on her hip.

"In the lobby."

Did she just call me a dimwit? Sam sucked in his lips to hide a grin.

Sophie waved her hand like she was shooing flies. "And I'll get the rest myself, thank you very much."

His lips turned up in a slight smile—still adorable when she was mad. And her fiery red-headed self hadn't changed.

He stepped into the lobby with the bags. Was her heart beating as rapidly as his? Did she remember their first date for coffee and walk along the river? Or their kayak ride? What about their first kiss? Her lips were so soft next to his. He shook his head. He didn't deserve her. Not after what he had done.

He stroked his beard. He was pretty sure he was the last person she wanted to see after what he'd done. But it had been three years. She had to have moved on. Sam set the bag down on the lobby coffee table and his eyes fell on the tree. By the wine-colored wing tipped chair. The one she had sat on when he proposed. He shook his head.

"Daddy, come on." Darby tugged on his arm. "It's snowing. Can we go out in it?"

Sam looked outside. The flakes were clumping together as they drifted through the amber lights of the carport. This little girl was a good distraction. He was not ready to see Sophie. She must think he was an absolute jerk.

"It's getting dark, sweetheart. And you're not dressed for it."

"I can get dressed. It won't take very long. Come on."

Who could resist those big blue puppy dog eyes? She tugged on his arm till he followed her up the stairs to their room.

Sam sat on the edge of the bed while Darby yanked out her pink snow pants and gloves.

"Want help?"

"I can do it my own self." She sat on the floor and put one leg in and then the other. Her foot got stuck on the elastic cuff. She squinched up her face like she was going to win a competition.

Sam reached out to help her, but she managed to get her foot through.

"Good job, Darby Doo." He tugged her knit hat on and patted her on the head.

Now the trick would be to get downstairs without having to pass Sophie. And what were all those bags for, anyway?

Fifteen minutes had been long enough to get the snow bug out of Darby. She shivered as she ran towards the front door. A girl dressed as an elf met them with towels to clean their boots.

"Looks like you had fun. Did you like the snow?" She toweled off the remaining flakes on Darby's jacket.

"I love it." Her teeth chattered. "But it's so cold!" She hugged herself.

"You look like a girl who could use some hot chocolate. There's a table next to the fireplace with cookies and drinks. That is, if it's okay with your dad." She smiled.

"Yes, of course." Darby ran to the table.

"Just one cookie, doodle. Take your pick." Sam took a cup and filled it with cocoa from a carafe. He squirted whipped cream from the can and handed it to Darby. "Sit down here so you don't spill."

She took a bite out of a gingerbread man and carefully set her cup on the table. Sam looked at the activity board. There were daily activities for kids of all ages. He'd sign her up and maybe go with the adults on the planned cross-country ski trip. He could use some adult time.

Sam loved the role of dad. But he could use a break now and then. It had been a crazy ride. The phone call that his brother Henry and sister-in-law, Theresa had been in a car accident. Rushing to the hospital only to find Theresa had died. A few final hours with his brother, where he asked Sam to promise to parent two-year-old Darby.

"All done? Throw your napkin and cup away. Let's get you into bed. Got some fun things for you to do tomorrow."

They reached the room where he drew a warm bath, pulled out her fuzzy fleece Christmas jammies with the polar bears, and brushed through her straight blonde hair.

"Read to me." She jumped up onto the bed and gave Sam a copy of The Kissing Hand. She snuggled her own stuffed Chester raccoon on her lap.

"Now," Mrs. Raccoon told Chester, "Whenever you feel

lonely and need a little loving from home, just press your hand to your cheek and think," here, Darby chimed in.

"Daddy loves you." She put her hand on her cheek and snuggled closer to Sam.

Sam swallowed the lump in his throat. "And that kiss will jump to your face and fill you with toasty warm thoughts." How had he been the one to receive such a gift?

He kissed the top of her head. "Okay doodle, time for bed." He tucked her in, kissing her on each dimple just like daddy H did. "Sweet dreams. God bless you, baby girl."

Chapter Three

Sophie grabbed a wheeled luggage rack and filled it with the bags. She didn't owe him anything, especially not a conversation unless, of course, he was ready to give her the excuse she deserved for him leaving and never coming back. Suddenly hot, she unwound her scarf and threw it on top of the bags. Why in the world did this have to be the one week she would run into that man. It was bad enough that he had broken their engagement with a text. *A text!* Who even does that? And obviously he was married with a kid.

She shoved the luggage rack a little harder than needed, managing to catch her scarf in the wheels. Sophie huffed out an exasperated breath and untangled it. She moved into the activity room and began emptying her goodies, arranging them by each day's activity. Thank goodness this was a large resort. She shouldn't have any trouble avoiding him. Or his full beard. Or mesmerizing eyes. One glance was all it took to remember what loving him had been like.

Letting these thoughts worm their way in was not okay. The man was married. And he obviously hadn't wanted her in his life. Just as well. If he was willing to walk away form a two-year relationship, then he wasn't the man she thought he was in the first place. She didn't need him. She was doing just fine.

Sophie pulled out her colored markers and drew a festive border around the white board. She colored in the berries on the holly leaves and stood back to admire her work. She would do what she did best—throw herself into her work with kids. She would just ignore the fact that he was here. No sense getting her tinsel in a tangle.

She wrote the days of the week, and the lists of activities. Tomorrow they would build snowmen. She looked out the window where white flakes continued to fall. There should be plenty of snow by then.

She arranged piles of plastic carrots, large buttons, scarves, mittens and. . . She put her finger on her chin. Some sticks for arms would be nice. She could look for those early the next morning. She looked at her bag of ribbons. She should take those too. Maybe the kids could think of something creative to do with them. Who knew? Kids always came up with interesting things. She checked the time. Better turn in. Hopefully tomorrow she'd be so wrapped up in the fun of kids that she'd forget all about Sam.

Sophie slid the key card into the door of her room just as her phone chimed. "Hey! Claire. You are just the person I need to talk to." She slid her bag from her shoulder and onto the dresser.

"What's going on? Everything okay?"

"I wish. It was great, until..." Sophie kicked off her ankle boots, sending one flying across the room.

"Until what? What's going on?"

Sophie sat down against the pillows on her bed. "Three guesses as to who is here." Silence.

"You there?" She crossed her legs at the ankles.

"Yeah, I'm thinking."

"I was unloading my car with all the activity supplies and who should offer to help me? Sam!"'

"Shut up."

"Yes. Can you believe it? Here our trip to Europe is ruined by the strike and now my whole Christmas week is going to be ruined." Sophie wound a strand of hair around her finger so tight the end was turning purple.

"Woah now. It's gonna be okay. Take a breath."

"I'm not taking a breath. He has a kid! A little girl! The jerk's married!"

"Oh my gosh. Sophie. I don't even know what to say. What's his wife like?"

"I don't know. I didn't see her."

"Did you talk to him? Did he apologize?"

"Are you kidding? I just told him to put the bag down in the lobby. I wasn't going to give him the time of day."

"How did he look?"

"Tall. Bushy beard. Handsome. Come on Claire. Don't make me do this." Sophie put her hand on her forehead.

"I always liked him. You need to talk to him. Let him explain. Maybe he had a perfectly good reason for breaking it off."

"Are you kidding? He could have at least done me the favor of explaining— an email. A phone call. In two years of a relationship, wasn't I worth that much?" Sophie rolled her shoulders. A hot bath was sounding really good.

"Yes, you were worth it. You still are. Take a breath. Hot bath. Bubbles. Watch a movie. I'll call you later."

Sophie awoke, not feeling as rested as she would have hoped. Too many thoughts squirreling around her mind. *Please tell me it isn't true. That was someone else I saw last night.*

She dressed in a pair of jeans and a red sweatshirt with ~~Best~~ Worst Christmas Pageant Ever written on the front and a picture of a girl with hair shooting out all over her head.

Sophie grabbed a chocolate glazed croissant from the lobby table and held it in her mouth as she secured her knit scarf. The snow had stopped falling, but it was still cold. She searched around the yard and made a stack of suitable snowman arms, then made her way inside.

Just in time to see Megan, dressed as an elf coming down the hall followed by a dozen boisterous kids.

"Do you want me to lead them to the activity room?"

"Would you? That would be great. I'm going to start with story time."

Megan placed name tags on each of the kids and sat them on the carpet.

"I am so glad you're here today!" She eyed each child's name tag and welcomed them. *Wait. Wasn't that the girl with Sam last night? His daughter?* She swallowed.

"Uh, hi Darby. Glad you could come today." *Those big eyes. And dimples. She didn't remember Sam having dimples. Must have gotten them from her mom.* Sophie blinked.

"We're going to start with a story and then head outside to make a snowman. Sound okay to you?" Choruses of *yes* and *yay* echoed off the walls.

Sophie and Megan helped the smaller kids put on their gloves and then carried totes full of supplies for their snow people.

"I can help. Let me help carry that."

Sophie looked down.

"Uh, sure, Darby. Take one side of the tote."

Darby heaved it.

"Are you sure it's not too heavy?"

"I can do it. My dad says I'm really strong." *Yeah, I bet he does.*

They headed to the back where the snow was thickest. It covered the branches, leaving small bits of green peeking out. A cardinal sat on a branch, its red plumage contrasting against the white.

The sun sparkled on the snow "Miss Sophie, it's like diamonds!" *Diamonds. Yeah. About that.*

Sophie directed the older kids to help the younger with forming their snowballs and they soon had a group of snow people awaiting faces and features.

Sophie walked slowly by each one, remarking on the placement of the eyes, their beautiful scarves and crazy branch arms. She came to Darby's and let out a giggle. "You used ribbons and made hair for yours. That's cute."

"I made it long and red. See I made someone pretty to marry my daddy— just like you, Miss Sophie." *Woah now. What? He's not married?*

"Well, it's very cute. I'm sure your daddy will love it." *Can't wait to see what he thinks of that.*

Chapter Four

"Room service." A rap on her door. Sophie let the teen wearing reindeer antlers in. She took the tray with her bowl of beef stew and slice of French bread and placed it on the table.

"Will there be anything else?"

"No, this is great. Thanks." Sophie was not interested in taking the chance of running into Sam in the restaurant. Not now. Not ever. She'd gotten through day one at least. Six more to go. She could do this.

Unbid memories snuck into her mind. She and Sam had met in a hardware store of all places. She had been looking for something to stop her toilet from running. He had helped her pick out the toilet kit and offered to fix it for her. And standing at the doorway, watching him fix it like a pro, his broad shoulders and muscular arms in fluid motion. Who knew she would see a guy as a hero just because he fixed her toilet?

Sophie took a bite of her stew and stared out the window. The setting sun shot streams of light through the snow-covered branches. It had been such a fun day. Seeing the laughter, creativity and smiles on the kids was the bee's knees. She couldn't think of a better profession.

She checked Pinterest for a few more ideas for the next day's activities and pinned shots of today's snowmen. She had to admit, Darby was a cutie. Not as cute as she and Sam would have had together, but. . . Nope. She would not let herself go there. It was over.

She stretched, changed into a pair of sweats. She grabbed the fuzzy throw that was on the couch, her new Christmas book and headed down for a cup of hot cocoa. She slurped some of the whip cream, and cradled the cup in both hands, her throw around her shoulders and book under her arm. She started for the couch by the fireplace, but then she saw all the Christmas lights shining outside. It would be more fun to sit on the deck. It should be warm enough. The lodge crew had thought of everything. A fire pit was blazing, and tall patio heaters stood next to each Adirondack chair.

She backed out of the glass door and caught sight of Sam. He had his guitar and was strumming chords to *Silent Night*. Her heart raced. Making a sudden retreat, she tripped on her blanket. She let out a squeal. Sam jumped out of the chair and ran to catch her. Her breath caught at the woodsy scent of him as he wrapped his arms around her. Hot chocolate and whip cream spilled on them both.

He stepped back. "Are you okay? Let me help you clean that up."

She pulled away. "Thanks, but no thanks. I don't *need* your help."

Sam started to wipe up spilled cocoa with her blanket. Sophie let it fall to the ground and turned to go back inside.

"Wait. Sophie." He stood and reached for her elbow.

Her gaze swept over his face.

"I'm really sorry about how I ended things."

Sophie turned. "A text, Sam? Really? You couldn't have called or emailed?"

Sam hung his head. "I know. I was a real coward."

Sophie crossed her arms. Claire had said to hear him out. Well then, she would give him five minutes.

"I lost my job. I didn't think you would want a guy who couldn't provide for you."

"I bet your boss had the decency to tell you in person." She shook her head. "And that wasn't a decision you had a right to make for me." Her voice was sharp. She turned. "Nice to see you've moved on. What a great place to spend with your family. I find it odd that you'd take them where you proposed to me." This conversation was through. She grabbed the wet blanket and slammed through the door.

Sam watched her go, her long red curls bouncing on her back. The same red hair he had loved to run his hands through when he kissed her. He swallowed. Her words pricked at his heart. She was right. He hadn't given her the chance to make that decision. He sat back down and warmed his hands by the flame. He picked up his guitar and mindlessly strummed chords. He couldn't undo what he'd done. But he wasn't the same man anymore. How could he let her know that?

After he had lost his job, he had faced the wrath of his parents, not able to live it down once they knew.

"Here we spent good money for you to go to college and get your accounting degree. And you had a good job. A great job. Your dad pulled strings to get you in with that team."

Sam knew he could have gotten a job at any number of places on his own merit. But his parents were all about control. And they had made him feel so ungrateful and incapable that it had been easier to let them run his life and ignore who he really was.

The truth of the matter was, he had been laid off because the company was downsizing. It wasn't even his fault. And truth be told, accounting was not what made his heart sing.

His mind played back to every test he took to achieve his parents' ultimate goal of getting into the right college. If he went on a date, he had to have the right girl, from the right family, who wore the right clothes. It didn't matter if he didn't have feelings for her.

No matter what he did, he was never going to be worthy of their love.

Sam set his guitar down and watched the twinkle of the white lights wrapped around the trees. The moon had peeked through the clouds and shone on the snowmen. Darby had such a fun time today. She couldn't stop telling him all about the elf that picked her up, the other kids, building their snow-men. And Miss Sophie.

But what had she been thinking? A snow gal with long red hair like Sophie's? Who knew it would be Sophie leading the activities? This was supposed to be a fun get away with his little girl. But now? He wasn't so sure being around the only woman who had ever stolen his heart was a good thing.

Chapter Five

Sophie hummed along with *Sleigh Bells Ring* as she brushed her hair. She should put it up since they'd be making Christmas ornaments today.

"It's a beautiful night, we're happy and bright, walking in a winter wonderland." She pulled it back, twisted it into a bun and wrapped a snowflake printed scarf around her head. If only she *were* happy and bright. Did Sam not realize how his abrupt breakup had affected her? Did he think he could send one text and life would somehow magically just go on? And why was losing his job such a big deal? Sure, it hurts. And throws you off balance. But he could always get something else.

Her stomach rumbled. She couldn't spend every morning, noon and night worrying about running into him. She would just go to the buffet. There were plenty of people around. Surely, she wouldn't run into him. And that cute little girl.

She made her way down the spiral staircase, twinkle lights and garland wrapped around the log railing. The whole lodge was stunning. Coming here would make a Christmas believer out of anyone, Scrooge or not. The mantle over the stone fireplace held hand carved characters of the nativity. A round table was set in the lobby with puzzle pieces scattered around, awaiting those wanting to leisurely put the Christmas picture in place.

People seemed so peaceful and content, smiles on their faces. She wished the anxiety wrapping itself around her stomach would settle down. Not gonna happen so long as he was here. She picked up a plate and had a hard time deciding whether she wanted eggs and sausage, waffles, or fruit and yogurt, which was probably the best choice. But it was Christmas, after all. She took a crepe blintz with blueberries and whip cream, grabbed an iced chocolate chip cranberry scone for later and headed to the coffee pot. Nothing like a little comfort food.

She glanced around. Was it better to choose a table in the far back corner? But then, she'd have to walk through the whole place to the entrance and there was more of a chance of running into him. Oh, there was Megan.

"Mind if I join you?"

"Of course, sit here." Megan nodded her head towards the empty chair. Sophie went over the day's activity plans. Make ornaments out of popsicle sticks, take the kiddos out sledding on the hill out back, warm them up with hot cocoa.

"Megan, were you standing by the snowmen when Darby said she made a pretty snow gal like Miss Sophie, to marry her daddy?"

Megan laughed. "Yeah. She's so cute."

"But have you seen Darby's mom? When you picked the kids up? Or around here anywhere?"

"No, come to think of it. Maybe he's not married." Megan shrugged. "He is kinda hot."

Sophie felt warmth crawling up her cheeks. It must be the heat of the candle in the center of the table.

"Look at you. You think he is, don't you?" Megan gave her a soft punch on her arm.

Sophie stood up. "I'll go get things organized. See you in a few."

"It's gonna be a great day today, kids. We're making ornaments for the tree downstairs, then going sledding. Sound like fun?"

Sounds of cheering made her smile.

"Oh, and we're going to perform a Nativity play for your parents and guests on Christmas Eve. We'll need angels, shepherds, wise men, Mary, Joseph, some animals. And someone to hold the star."

Darby threw up her hand. "I want to be Mary."

Sophie scanned the room. She needed someone older for Mary. The costume she had was way too big for that little girl. Darby would be a good angel.

"I want to be Mary."

"Thank you, Darby. I'll be watching each of you and assigning roles at the end of the day."

"Okay. Then you can tell me I'll be Mary." She turned to Micah next to her and linked arms. "And you can be Joseph!"

Micah gave a slow nod, his smile showing his missing front teeth.

"On the table are some colored popsicle sticks, glitter, string and hot glue guns. You need to be careful and let Miss Megan or I help with the hot glue. But first, I want you to draw a picture of you and your family to go in the stick frame."

Sophie turned on some kids' Christmas music and wandered around to help.

Sam hopped in his pickup. Darby had been hyper all morning, counting the minutes till she could be with Miss Sophie doing activities. She wouldn't miss it for the world.

He followed the van over the newly plowed road up the mountain. Trees were laden with fresh snow, and it covered the landscape in soft hills. Going on a snowshoe hike with the other adults would be a good diversion.

Would there ever be a chance to explain where life had taken him? She needed to know that he was not the same man as before. If fate didn't push them together, he was going to make sure he crossed paths with Sophie today.

Sam parked his truck, filled with all the snowshoes.

"Here, let me help you with those." Justin started handing snowshoes to each participant.

"The weather is perfect. A few light clouds. And the snow is just powdery enough."

"How long have you worked at the Lodge?" Sam pulled the tailgate down for a bench.

"About five years. It's a really fun job." Justin buckled his snowshoes and stood, watching to see that everyone got their straps tightened. "You look familiar. Have you stayed here before?"

"Yeah, actually. I was here a few years ago."

"Oh. I remember you now. You had that really cute girl-friend with the red hair. Wait, she's the one we hired for kids' activities, isn't she?"

Sam swallowed. "Yeah. My daughter's in her classes. She's loving it." Justin waved everyone to follow him and gave some instructions.

"She was a lucky catch for you."

Yes, she was. Had been. "We're not together anymore."

"What? She must have ditched you. You wouldn't have

been crazy enough to let her go." Justin laughed and glanced at Sam.

"I wish that were true." Sam dug his pole into the snow a little harder than he needed to.

"Woah dude. Do you want to talk about it?"

They took a few more steps.

"I broke it off. In a text." *The pain in her eyes. But he had done it for her.*

"Dude." Justin stopped and stared at him. "I don't think I've ever done anything that dumb."

And I wish I could say the same. "I don't know. I panicked. I got laid off and was afraid I couldn't provide for her, you know, give her the life she deserved."

"So, I'm guessing you didn't know she was here? That must be awkward."

"You're telling me. A lot has changed since then. I've got some explaining to do."

"Were you guys, like, engaged?"

Sam remembered when he told her—*I can't imagine ever living without you.*

"Yup."

"So, have you moved on? Or do you still love her?"

Did he? Absolutely. That Sophie shaped hole in his heart that was never filled. The question was, would she let him back in?

Sam clenched his jaw.

"You do. I can see it all over your face. Talk to her man. You gotta get this worked out. I'll be rooting for you."

Okay Lord. Are you going to be rooting for me too? Was this your crazy way of bringing us back together?

Chapter Six

Darby stood next to Sophie in the activity room, her pigtails sticking cockeyed in an unruly array. Sam had made an attempt at beauty skills, but with that straight, fine, blonde hair he had to work with, he thought it was a miracle she looked as good as she did.

He watched as Sophie tried to straighten them out. His face contorted in a scowl. What was she doing? He didn't need her help. How his daughter's hair looked wasn't a matter of life or death.

"Hey Darby Doodle, ready to go?"

Darby ran and threw her arms around her dad.

"How was your day?"

Darby pulled back and crossed her arms. She glared at Sophie.

"That mean Miss Sophie won't let me be Mary in the baby Jesus play. I told her that's who I wanted to be, but she won't let me." An alligator tear rolled down her eye.

"Wait, a Nativity play? That sounds fun."

"It won't be. She's mean. I hate her!" Darby stomped her foot.

"Come on now. That's not the way to be." He wiped her tear with his thumb. "Sometimes things don't always work out the way we want them to." Sam glanced up and realized Sophie was standing there. With her arms crossed. With a look that could only mean *did you really just say that?*

Now would be a good time to leave. "Get your coat. Did you do any projects we need to take?"

"Yeah, I made a ornment." She ran to her cubby and retrieved it. "See, I made daddy H, mama T and this is you and this is me." She threw on a proud grin.

"Daddy H and mama T?" Sophie stepped near them.

Sam looked up. "Darby, go get your coat. I'll be right with you." He turned to Sophie. "Daddy Henry and mama Teresa." He sat down on the edge of the child sized table. "Henry was my older brother. They were in a tragic car accident."

Sophie's mouth formed an O and she put her hand on his shoulder. "That's awful." She sat down beside him. "How old was Darby?"

"Yes, it was. Horrible. She was two. Teresa died immediately. Henry asked me to raise her if he didn't make it." His face clouded.

Sophie placed her hand on his. The warmth of her compassion travelled to his heart. Oh, how he had missed her.

"So, you've been raising her the last two years?"

"Yep. For a while I really questioned whether it was a good idea or not. There were more than a few times she would have been better off with someone else." *Who did I think I was to raise a kid? I couldn't even have a successful relationship.* "Thank goodness they had her potty trained. Not that she didn't revert back to diapers for a while. She's a good kid. I feel really blessed to have her. We had to learn together—feel each other out. Figure out what it was like to be a pair. She's changed my life." Sam stole a glance at the stunning woman beside him. His heart pushed out a strained beat. Sophie was so beautiful it hurt. He wanted to reach out and touch her. Why oh, why had he broken it off? He swallowed. *I need to be careful here. I can't just think of myself. I have to think of Darby first.*

"Did your parents help out?"

"My folks help out now and then. They stop by long enough for my dad to tell me all the things I'm doing wrong." *All I ever wanted from him was praise and him to be proud of me.*

"So, nothing's changed with them, huh?" Her lips had a tug of a smile.

He nodded.

She adjusted the scarf on her head. "Remember that time when we stopped by their house to borrow a hammer so I could hang pictures in my apartment?"

"And my dad told me I didn't know the handle from the claw?"

They laughed.

"And you held the nail while I hammered. You were pretty brave."

He remembered the scent of her hair rubbing against his bare arm.

Sam cleared his throat and glanced at Darby who was drawing a picture. "After I lost my job, Henry took me on as a carpenter apprentice. That's what I do now. I really like it."

"Maybe losing your job didn't turn out to be a bad thing."

The only bad thing about it was losing you.

"What are you doing now?" He looked into her hazel eyes. The touch of her hand was still warm on his.

"I've been subbing for a second-grade class while the teacher is on maternity leave. I was hoping to get hired full time, but it's really hard to get on at that school. So, I've applied for a dream job at an international school."

"You always liked to travel. And I'm sure you're a good teacher. Darby loves you."

"In spite of not being Mary. The truth is, I only have so many costumes and the one for Mary is way too large for her. She'll make a great angel."

"She'll get over it. She doesn't hold a grudge for very long." Sam stood and glanced at Darby who was chasing Micah around the room. "Come on Darby. Grab your picture and coat. We need to get some dinner."

"I want to ask a favor of you. Would you be willing to play guitar for us? We want to sing *Away in a Manger* and it would be way better with an instrument."

Sam turned. "Uh yeah. I guess I could do that. Tomorrow?"

Sophie nodded.

Sophie walked outside, zipped up her down jacket and pulled her knit hat tighter. The night couldn't have been more gorgeous—cold and clear filled with more stars than she could count. Orion's belt sparkled and led her eyes to the big dipper. She flashed to Sam holding her hand to pointing out the constellations. She sighed. Would there be any chance they could get together again? The way he had talked to her this afternoon. Well, she had to admit it was softening her heart.

She couldn't imagine taking on a two-year-old like he had. Losing his brother and sister-in-law would have been enough trauma. But to try to hold it together for a sweet little girl? She had never seen that coming. Not that he hadn't liked kids, but they weren't really in his realm. Kids were her gig. But even with that, could she have taken on the challenge of raising a young niece?

Sophie's boots crunched through the top layer of snow as

she walked towards the hillside. It was lit with hundreds of patio lights strung between poles and large bright lights as seen at night construction sites. Kids and adults were sledding down, squeals of laughter and happy voices. She couldn't help joining the joy with a laugh that escaped her lips.

Suddenly, a sled with a bundled-up girl with a red nose holding tightly to a stuffed raccoon slid by her, narrowly missing her feet. Sophie yelped and jumped back.

"Miss Sophie!"

"Well now, you look like you're having fun."

"Yeah, me 'n Chester love sledding." Darby jumped off the sled, placed Chester on it and grabbed onto the rope. "You should go down with me! It's really fun."

"I don't know." Sophie looked around. Sam must be around somewhere. This could be a little awkward.

"Come on. I know you'll like it." Darby grabbed her hand and started tugging on her.

"Okay, maybe one ride." She followed Darby up the hill. "Who is your raccoon?"

"Chester. You know. From *The Kissing Hand*? The story where his mom kisses the raccoon's hand and tells him he can always feel her kiss when she puts it on her cheek?" Darby stopped, made Chester give her a kiss on her mitten and put it onto her cheek. She smiled.

"I do know that story." *Is that how Sam has taught her to remember her mom and dad?*

They reached the top where Sam was waiting.

"You're going sledding too?"

Sophie nodded.

"Well hop on. Darby, you sit in front with Chester."

Sophie climbed onto the sled and put her arms around Darby's waist. Behind her, a light flashed. Did Sam just snap a photo?

"Ready girls?" Sam crouched down and gave Sophie's back a shove. Sophie squealed, held tighter to Darby and not even a minute later, laughed as they reached the bottom of the short hill.

"That was fun, Miss Sophie! Didn't you think so?" Darby hopped off and held her hand to Sophie to help her up. *Someone's been teaching her good manners.*

"Let's do it again." Darby held Sophie's hand as Sophie drug the sled up the hill.

"Daddy! Chester and I can stay up here while you and Miss Sophie go down." Sophie hesitated and looked at Sam.

"Come on! You have to!" Darby squealed. "Besides, friends don't let friends sled alone."

Sophie allowed Sam to give her a hand as she settled in to the front and he slid in behind her. He rested his hands on her shoulders and dug his feet into the snow to push them off the slope. He moved his hands around her waist. She stiffened. This shouldn't be happening. The pain of rejection hit her. But before they hit the bottom her head was leaning against his chest.

Sam swerved to avoid another sled and upturned theirs where it stopped. Sophie face planted and heard a deep, rumbling laughter. She pushed herself up and stood planting her hands on her hips and a frown on her face.

"Thanks a lot Sam!" He let out another laugh.

"You should see yourself! There's snow all over your face."

He pulled off his gloves and reached over to flick snow off her eyelashes. His touch undid her when he let his fingers linger. Time stopped as as she gazed into his eyes.

Sophie's heart began to race. "It's really cold out here." She had to remember what he had done to her. She couldn't let herself get pulled into his touches. "I'm going in to get some hot cocoa." *Don't look at his eyes. Or his lips. Or think about kissing him. Nope. Not gonna let him hurt me again.*

"Yeah. Good idea. I'll get Darby and join you in a minute."

Chapter Seven

"Hold still, Darby. I can't put your hair in a pony while you're wiggling around."

"Sorry, daddy. You should have brought the vacuum. Then you could make a good pony like at home."

Sam chuckled. It was true, he had sucked her straight blond hair into the vacuum and slid the tie around it. It had been a whim and had made her laugh at a time when they were doing more crying than not.

"There. How does that look?" He turned her around to face the mirror.

"Do you think angels wear ponytails? Or would they get in the way of the halo?"

"Now that's a good question, little girl. I've never thought of that. Hop down now. Miss Megan elf will be here soon to pick you up."

Darby squealed and ran to get her coat.

That morning Sam had agreed to help Justin build a makeshift stable for the play. It shouldn't take that long, and he'd still have time to bring his guitar to practice with the kids.

The sun rose, shining bright spots on the spectacular snow-covered mountain ridge. Sam's thoughts drifted to last night. Sledding had been such fun. Reminded him of the time they had tobogganed and ended the night with cocoa and peppermint straws. And hugs. And goodnight kisses. Long goodnight kisses.

He shook his head. *If* there was a chance of them getting together again, he knew one thing for certain. He would never let her go. How could he have been so self-absorbed?

"Hey Sam—" Justin handed him a cup of steaming coffee. "Let's throw these two by fours together for the base. I've already cut them to size. Then we can top them off with plywood for a bit of a stage first."

"Good plan." Sam picked up a cordless drill and threw some screws in a plastic tub.

"Looked like you might have been having some fun last night. I watched you through the window where it was warm and toasty." Justin lined the two by fours along the floor like a puzzle.

"Yeah. Darby loves sledding. She could have stayed out there all night. That little girl has a lot of energy. She gives me a run for my money." He laughed and screwed two pieces together.

"How about that big girl that joined you? Looked like there was some fun going on there too."

Sam felt his cheeks grow warm. "Yup." He looked up when he heard hurried footsteps.

It was the receptionist. "Hey, there's a girl stuck in the snow out front. She tried to get out without chains. Do you think you could go help her?"

Sam nodded at Justin. He checked the time. They left their tools and followed her out. A college aged girl had her down magenta ski coat zipped up and a purple cable knit scarf tucked around her neck. Her hair was twirled around in a top bun and a matching wide headband covered her forehead and ears. She rubbed her gloved hands together in front of her steamy breath.

Sam walked around the car, put his gloved finger to his chin.

"Why don't you go on into the lobby. There's coffee, hot chocolate. A fire. Get yourself warm while we take care of your car." She gave Sam a wide smile.

It took Sam's truck and a winch to pull her car to level ground. Tag teaming it, Sam and Justin connected the tire chains in short order. Sam anxiously checked the time. Not short enough.

"Okay everybody. Mary, you and Joseph come stand at the side. Animals—that means donkey, sheep, cow, come stand behind the manger. Who has the star?"

"I do, Miss Sophie." Christina held the rod high with a foil covered star attached to the top. She started to walk to the manger, letting the stick rise and dip nearly hitting Justin.

"Watch out, little miss. Hold it high."

"Can we wear our costumes now Miss Sophie? It will be much more funner."

"I suppose so, Elaine. Miss Megan can hand them out." Sophie looked at the time. She needed to get the kids organized and at least do one run through before Sam got here to lead singing.

She tugged an angel costume over Darby's head, fastened the back and helped her on with her wings. "You make a great angel. Wanna see?" She held the camera on her phone towards her. Darby turned slightly to get a view of her wings.

"But where's my halo? I has to have a halo." Sophie laughed.

"Yes, you do." She looked in the box and pulled out a headband with a sparkling halo attached.

"Okay, let's try this again. Everyone line up." Sophie stood back, folded her arms and looked over everything. This was going to be sweet. Sure to bring some smiles.

"It would be nice to have an actual manger. I don't think it would be that hard to build."

"My daddy could build it. He's a carpenter, just like Jesus!" Darby jumped up and down, skewing her halo.

Speaking of which, he should be here in a few more minutes. "Let's practice *Away in a Manger* before Darby's dad gets here. Remember the hand motions?"

They started in, their sweet voices melding together. She hoped Jesus didn't get tired of hearing that song every year.

This was so much better than going to Europe for Christmas. Creating memories with kids and their families. This week must have been planned by someone bigger than her. Someone who knew what she needed. She felt her cheeks grow red remembering Sam's fingers on her eyelids last night.

She looked at the time again. Why wasn't he here? She had said eleven o'clock, right? It was eleven forty-five. Had he stood her up? Well, it wouldn't be the first time. She rounded up the kids, placing their costumes back in the tub and gave them each the snowflakes they had made earlier to take to their parents. She held the door open for them to make their way back to their parents.

"Daddy!" Darby ran and threw herself into Sam's arms. "Where were you?" Sam gave her a quick hug and made his way to Sophie, whose narrowed eyes shot daggers.

"I am so sorry."

"You forgot about us, didn't you? When you said you'd be here today, I took that as a promise." Sophie crossed her arms.

"I didn't forget." Sam lifted his baseball cap and ran his hand through his dark hair. "First I was helping Justin build a stage for you. And then we got interrupted by the desk clerk. There was a girl who ran her car off the side of the road and needed chains and help digging out."

Her eyes were like the flames in the lobby fireplace.

"And I suppose that was more important than being here for your daughter." *And me.*

Sam looked down. "Look, I'm really sorry. I was all set to be here on time and then we got started with her car and I didn't remember till we were through."

"Yeah. Okay. Fine." Sophie turned her back on him and started picking up the room.

"Keeping a commitment couldn't possibly have been one of the reasons you lost your job." Her voice just above a whisper. She didn't look at Sam. She couldn't.

"Daddy, let's go. I'm hungry. And daddy, you has to make a Jesus box for our play."

Yeah, we'll see how that goes. Not gonna count on it.

Chapter Eight

S ophie let the hot water run through her hair relaxing her tight shoulders. What would make her think he would have carried out what he said he would? It was a simple request. And if nothing else, it was for his daughter for Pete's sake. She poured shampoo onto her hand and rubbed it through her long strands. She could get by just fine without a manger. She didn't even really need a stage. Let him go sit on a pinecone. With sharp edges.

She dried off and wrapped a towel around her head. Why Lord? This could have been a perfectly peaceful week without throwing him in here. She threw a pillow onto the floor and fell on her stomach.

He was a good guy. He had always been impulsive when it came to helping someone. When his elderly neighbor was out of kindling, he was there, chopping it for her. When a new family had moved in across the street, he was the first to bring a pizza and offer to help. It just seemed like helping others always came first before her. She had never been able to accept that. She deserved a man who could put her above everyone else. Lay down his life for her.

She sat up. What am I thinking? He isn't Jesus! The man was allowed to have *some* flaws.

"Daddy."

Sam held Darby's hand as they walked back to their room.

Sophie was right. He *had* put someone else's needs above hers. Above Darby's. All the more reason not to re-engage in a relationship. Even though his eyes craved to take in every bit of her. Her fiery green eyes. Curly red hair. That little bit of a turned-up nose. Nope. He was not going to allow himself to take in her beauty. It would only complicate things.

He had Darby to think about. Sophie wasn't going to want to be saddled down with a little girl. She had her own life to live.

"Daddy. I'm trying to talk to you." Darby moved to face him and crossed her arms.

"Sorry, doodle." He crouched down to eye level. "What's up?"

"You gots to make the manger. I think you hurt Miss Sophie's feelings."

"You're right." He ruffled her hair. "Let's get some dinner and you can help me build it." He swallowed.

Darby had finished her mac and cheese and was licking a strawberry ice cream cone. Sam's eyes scanned the restaurant and was relieved to not see a shock of long red hair.

"Come on, Darby. I need my little assistant to help me with this project. We'll finish the stable first and then put together the manger." They headed to the shop where the tools still lay scattered from earlier.

"Do you need a screwdriver or the hammer?" Darby held the tools, one in each hand.

Sam held up a screw. Darby set the hammer down and sat

on the base. Sam held the screw while Darby used both hands to line up the drill.

"Go easy on it now. Not too fast or you'll get my fingers."

Darby pressed the button and expertly drilled the screw into the wood.

"I'm going to have to hire you out, little miss. I think you've found your calling." He gave her a side hug.

"Just doing what you taught me." She beamed at him.

Sam slid a sheet of plywood onto the base while Darby brought the box of screws.

"Hey!" Sophie leaned against the doorway— a knit shawl wrapped around her. Sam looked up. "Do you want some help? I'm not bad with a skill saw."

Was this an olive branch?

"I was just getting the flooring lined up. Come push on the front while I adjust the side. Darby, bring the drill and screws over here."

"I wanted to apologize for getting mad earlier today." She fiddled with the pendant hanging around her neck. "I shouldn't have lashed out at you."

"Accepted." Was she still wearing the sapphire necklace he had given her that Christmas?

"Daddy, is it okay if I hold the screw and Miss Sophie drills? I'm getting kinda tired."

"Sure, doodle."

"Do you know how to do it, Miss Sophie? The button is here. Go slow so you don't screw my fingers."

"Okay, I think I've got this." Sophie shared a grin with Sam.

"Thanks, Miss Sophie. Daddy, can I watch a movie on your phone? This hard work is pooping me out."

Sam pulled his phone out of his hip pocket and handed it to her. She crawled onto the couch and snuggled under a blanket.

"She's cute, Sam. You're really lucky to have her in your life. I bet she brings you a lot of joy."

"That she does. She's pretty much my everything. I don't know what I'd do if anything ever happened to her."

Sophie put her hand on Sam's arm. "Sam, thank you for doing this." She motioned towards the stable. "It means a lot."

"No problem. I love working with wood. Creating things. The satisfaction of seeing completed projects."

"I never really saw you as an accountant. It seemed, I don't know, too stiff. Too predictable."

"Yeah, well, I've learned a lot about myself in the last few years." Sam hoped she could see that he wasn't the same man. That he had changed. Besides having a job he loved, he made decent money. And he had taken on Darby Doo. That had to count for something, right?

"Hey Darby, doin' okay?"

"Yes, daddy. I'm the epi-dome of coz. My blanket's all fuzzled up on me."

He let out a chuckle. He turned to Sophie, drinking in her smile as she gazed at Darby. It seemed to be more than just a smile. Was there longing there?

"What do you think of this old barn wood for the manger?"

"Perfect!"

Sam measured the support pieces and penciled an angle. He handed Sophie the skill saw. She put on safety glasses and lined up the cut while Sam held the end of the board in place.

"Do you remember when I taught summer camp in Germany?"

Sam nodded.

"There was a man who made all these amazing carvings—nutcrackers, intricate tree ornaments, even a star for the top of the tree. It was so fun to watch him take a plain piece of wood and turn it into something beautiful. I always wished I had bought something from him and brought it home."

"I've done a bit of whittling. It's fun. Here—hold these two pieces together."

Sophie twisted her hair into a braid and leaned in. Sam closed his eyes a moment while he breathed in the scent of her hair. His eyes dipped to her lips and darted back to the screw. It would be so easy to touch his lips to hers. To slip back in love with her. Who was he kidding? He had never been *out* of love with her.

Sam glanced at the couch where Darby was sleeping, his cell phone resting on her tummy. He should get her to bed so she'd be rested in the morning.

"Better call it a night. That little nugget needs her beauty rest." Sophie nodded.

"Still need me to bring my guitar tomorrow?" If only he could hold on to her gorgeous smile.

Chapter Nine

The espresso machine spurted steam as the barista filled Sophie's cup with extra hot coffee, chocolate syrup, orange peel and topped it with whip cream. Sophie adjusted her beanie and zipped her puff coat before taking the hot cup in her gloved hands. She stepped out the front door of the lodge to take a night walk around the property.

Her phone buzzed in her pocket. "Claire— you're up early."

"Just wanted to check in. How's everything going? You know with..."

"Okay. I have to admit I was pretty miffed at him the other day."

"What did he do?"

"He was supposed to bring his guitar to play with the kids during the play practice. And didn't show up."

"Typical."

"Yep. I'm afraid I gave him the old one-two verbal punch."

"He probably deserved it."

"That's just it. Turns out he had been helping some college

girl get her car out of the snowbank. Anyway, I apologized last night and helped him build a stable for the play."

"So, things are going okay then?"

Sophie took a sip of her coffee. "Yeah. I guess. I'm. . ."

"What?"

"I'm starting to have feelings for him again."

"Just be careful, sis. You don't need to have your heart broken again."

Sophie lined up the kids and stepped back with her cellphone. Sam strummed a few chords and began to sing.

"Away in a manger no crib for a bed. . ."

This was definitely post-worthy. Darby sang her little heart out, pigtails all askew.

And Sam's rich, deep voice. If she hadn't been right there, she'd have thought it was Josh Turner.

"The little Lord Jesus asleep on the hay." Sam set his guitar down and slid a grin towards Sophie.

"That was wonderful! What would you guys think if Mr. Sam played some other Christmas songs and we carol door to door?"

"Yay!" Sam shrugged a *why not* and helped line them up at the door.

"You definitely have a great gig here, working with these kids. You are really good at it."

Sam's hand was warm on her shoulder.

"Thank you. I love it. I really hope I get the international job. Some adventure and different kids to work with." She smiled.

Sam averted his eyes and moved his hand away. Maybe she shouldn't have said that. But let's be real here— why would she think there would be any chance of something between them again? She may as well continue her sights on that job. Get as far away from the guy who had ripped her heart out before she let him have a chance to do it again.

"We're hungry. All that singing wore us out." Darby held both hands on her stomach and leaned over.

"Well, you're in luck. I made some gingerbread cookie dough for us to roll out."

Megan had wiped the tables and set small balls of the ginger spiced dough at each place. She scooped a little flour for each and had a set of small rolling pins.

"Try to roll the dough evenly like this." Sophie demonstrated. "Then take your person cookie cutter and press it into the dough."

She watched them, the older kids helping the younger. Micah lifted his man, making him walk across the table to laughter. Until it crumpled.

"I'm just a cotton headed ninny muggings!" Micah let his head drop. Sophie hid a grin.

"You can roll him out again. No worries. When your cookie is ready, bring it over here to the toaster oven."

"Mine is ready, Miss Sophie." Darby slid it carefully onto her palm and walked to the oven.

"Nice job! Let's get this little guy into the oven to bake." Sophie slid open the door and when Darby placed her cookie on the tray, she pulled back her hand and let out a yowl.

"Ow, ow, ouch!" Big tears rolled down her cheeks.

"Oh no, let me see!" Sophie took her little hand and led her to the sink where she ran cold water on it.

"Megan, grab the first aid kit." Sophie sent a quick text to Sam.

<Darby burned her hand. Could you come?>

It was a matter of moments before Sam came bursting through the door.

"Where is she?"

Megan nodded her head towards Darby.

"Hey baby, let me see." Sam knelt to her level and took her hand. He glared at Sophie.

"What the heck were you doing? How did you let this happen?"

"Sam, I'm so sorry. We were baking cookies." Sophie reached her hand to his arm. Sam shrugged it off, picked up Darby and stomped off.

Sophie's shoulders dropped as she watched the man who had been her everything leave— her heart aching like it was breaking all over again. Just like it had all those years ago.

Chapter Ten

"Let's find all the straight edges first."

Darby sat on her knees at the table, as Sam helped her sort puzzle pieces.

"I found one with an ear. It's a dog, isn't it?" Darby held it carefully between her fingers, the gauze wrapped around her hand. She studied the photo on the box lid.

"Good job, doodle. Let's see if we can find another one with the same colors."

Flames flickered and crackled in the fireplace and soft Christmas instrumentals played in the background. The snow had started falling full force, covering the bushes and pathways. There were only four more days until Christmas. Sam wanted to enjoy this vacation time with his sweet girl. He could have, probably should have, planned to spend some holiday time with his folks. It was just that he always felt he had to defend himself for everything he did. He never felt he could live up to his dad's expectations. Henry had been his dad's favorite, something he couldn't ever tap into the reason of. Heck, Sam had gone to college like his dad had urged him to do. Henry had only done an apprenticeship. In his dad's eyes that shouldn't have been enough to give Henry a pat on the back. Nevertheless, Henry was, had been, the golden boy.

He couldn't blame his parents. Henry was full of fun and laughter, adventures, and surrounded by friends. Sam was more of an introvert. He shrugged and picked up another puzzle piece.

"Hey." Sophie's voice was soft as she slid up next to them. "I just wanted to see how Darby's hand was. May I sit down?"

Sam nodded.

Darby put her hand on Sophie's shoulder. "Miss Sophie, it's okay. It doesn't hurt anymore." Sam fit another puzzle piece together without looking up.

"I'm really sorry, Darby. I never wanted you to get hurt." Sophie stuck a stray strand of blonde hair behind Darby's ear. She picked up a piece with pink on it. "What do you think this is?"

"Don't you know? It's the doggie's nose, silly." Darby took the piece and rotated it until it fit in place.

Sam slid a glance at Sophie. He hadn't meant to lash out at her. He'd already ruined it for the two of them. But now he had caught himself thinking about Sophie way more than he ought. . . If there was any chance they were to get back together, he had to know that she would protect Darby no matter what.

Sam's phone vibrated. Sophie glanced at the screen. His mom.

"Hi mom." Sam stood and walked a few feet away. "What? No! Is he okay? What happened?" He put his hand on his forehead. "I can't go. There's a blizzard out there. I'm really sorry." Sam paced. "Keep me posted. I'll come as soon as the roads clear."

"Was that grandma?" Darby sat up on her knees.

"Yes."

"Everything okay?" Sophie stood, her forehead wrinkled.

"No. My dad had a mild stroke. He's at Mercy Hospital."

"And we're snowed in. Oh Sam, I'm so sorry. Maybe you could Facetime."

Sam pinched the bridge of his nose.

"Daddy, can I sit over there and watch the movie? It's Polar Express!"

"Sure. But don't go anywhere else, okay?"

Darby nodded and jumped off her chair to run to the couch.

"How are you doing, Sam? Are you okay?"

"I don't know. I feel guilty, but I would just as soon not see him. I'd get there, and if he could talk at all, he'd still manage to make sure I felt like gum on the bottom of his shoe."

Sophie stood and placed her hands on his shoulders, slowly rubbing the tight muscles.

"Maybe. But maybe this is the time when you could heal things."

"He's the one that has to do the healing, not me." Sam let out a slow breath and leaned into the table placing his head on his arms. He could feel the tightness begin in his shoulders.

The touch of her hands felt good. Too good. Memories of how things used to be flooded him. She moved her hands down his back and slowly up to his neck. Her thumbs kneaded the knots, and she moved her hands to his head, gently rubbing her fingers through his scalp. She leaned into his back and slid her hands down his chest, laying her cheek on the back of his head.

Sam sat up and moved his hands to hers. He breathed in the scent of her hair. His heart beat like it hadn't for so long.

"I've missed you Sam." He pulled her around to sit on his lap. He gathered her hair and smoothed it to her back. They locked eyes and he slid a glance to her open lips.

As if on cue, Darby barreled over to them. "Daddy, can I have some popcorn? They just made some, but Megan said I have to ask first." Darby stopped. Looked at them, her eyes wide.

Sophie quickly slid off his lap and ran her hand through her hair.

"Uh, I better get back and organize the gingerbread house contest."

Sophie sped to the stairs, her heart pounding. Did that just happen? Another second and he might have kissed her. She hitched a breath. Those dang butterflies in her stomach. They needed to get the memo that she and Sam were not a thing. Gingerbread. Need to get the houses ready. Focus!

Megan caught up with her. "Did I just see what I thought I did?"

"What?" Sophie looked straight ahead and kept walking.

"Mm hmm. That's what I thought. You almost kissed!"

Sophie opened the door to the activity room and started divvying candy onto cardboard matts.

"Christmas is in four days. And don't forget the Christmas Ball is in three. You're going, right?"

Sophie stopped and looked at her. "Could you just stop? I'm not ready for this."

Megan muttered, "Sure looked like you were."

Families began to filter in and take their places. She stood back and watched Sam and Darby pipe icing to place the house parts together. He let her choose gumdrops for the walkway and peppermints for the roof. When she broke open a bag of skittles and they went flying all over the floor and table, he just laughed and helped her pick them up, sorting them by colors. Darby lined up animal crackers.

"This is Chester. I'm going to make him live in the doggy

hotel." She took gummy bears and introduced them to Chester —Marshall, Rumble, Zuma, Skye.

He was a good dad. She wished his dad could see him now and appreciate how great he is. Then again, Sam was probably right. His dad might have turned things around to making him look a fool for allowing the candies to scoot everywhere. God, you could fix this though, right?

Chapter Eleven

The snow had finally ceased, and the full moon shone bright as day reflecting on the pure whiteness and casting shadows of the tall hemlocks. Sam had left Darby to play Chutes and Ladders with Justin's kids while he and Sophie donned snowshoes for an evening hike. He watched her hair sway with the movement of her hips. He tried not to look at her hips. He cleared his throat.

"You know, I did a little Facebook stalking awhile back and saw you had a boyfriend."

Sophie slowed and let him equal her stride. "You did what?" She slid a glance.

"Yeah. He looked like a football player—broad shoulders, tall. If I hadn't known better, I would have thought it was me." Sam smirked.

"Uh. Yeah. I guess Leo did look a bit like you."

"You still together?"

"Nah. I really wanted to like him. But. . ."

"But?"

Sophie turned. "Remember the time we went to see the zoo lights? We took photos in the tunnel of lights?"

How could he forget?

"And there was that six-foot blob fish light?" Sam blurted out and let out a snort.

"We did our best blob fish impressions." Sam pulled his lips back, forming his mouth like a fish. Sophie laughed hysterically. She caught hold of herself and matched his imitation. Sam let out a rumble, which started Sophie giggling so much she had to lean over to catch her breath. Sam pushed her shoulders back and she landed in the snow.

Sophie let out a surprised squeal. "You are so dead!" She grabbed a handful of snow, making a quick snowball and threw it at Sam.

He deflected, his arm covering his face.

"Oh, I see how it is."

He took a few steps back and gathered a snowball. Sophie dodged it, grabbed a handful of snow, and ran behind him. She jumped on his back and crammed it under his hoodie and down his back. She laughed as she slid back to the ground, adjusting her stance on her snowshoes.

He let out a scream and pulled his hoody off, shaking the snow out of it. Sam didn't miss her eyes working their way from his belly button slowly up to his lips.

She crossed her arms and stepped back. "We had planned to use the blob fish photos for our engagement photos." Her voice was soft.

Sam shook out his sweatshirt once more and slid it back on. Pain etched his face.

"I had to break up with Leo. He didn't fit the Sam shaped hole in my heart." She started to walk away. Sam caught up to her, turned her towards him and pulled her into his arms.

"Sophie."

She placed her hands on his biceps. He took a breath. His blue eyes searched hers.

"I am so sorry. I thought I would die without you, but I really believed I was doing the right thing. There has never been a day when I haven't thought about you and how stupid I was to let you go." He kissed her forehead. She stepped away and turned towards the lodge. "Where do you think things would be if things had worked out?"

"Happy. I'm not the one who ended it." She took a step. "You better get back to Darby. It's probably her bedtime and there's a big day ahead."

Sophie walked as quickly as she could, her snowshoes kicking up fluffy white puffs. Sam had Facebook stalked her? It wasn't like she hadn't done the same. Seen that there had been no sign of him dating again. Maybe there was hope for them.

Nope. This was a bad idea. She was just going to get hurt again. Why did he have to go and hug her? Stir up old memories of how good it felt to be in his arms. And his woodsy scent. Nope. She needed to stay as far away as possible. She'd just keep her head down and do her job. There were only a few more days anyway. She could make it through.

She sat on a bench in the drive through and removed her snowshoes, leaving them in a box to dry. Going into the lobby, she stopped by the coffee bar and made some hot cocoa to take to her room. She was ready to snuggle in a blanket and watch a cheesy Christmas movie. Alone. By herself. Ugh.

A woman that reminded her of her grandma stirred her cocoa beside her. "Isn't this place lovely? I just love it here."

"It is, for sure."

"And that full moon. So romantic." She took a sip of her cocoa, testing for taste.

"I saw you two out there. You looked like you were having fun. I could see love written all over your faces."

She waggled her eyebrows.

"I remember my Albert and I met here at Christmas, forty odd years ago."

Gotta get out of here.

Sophie began to walk away.

The woman put her hand on Sophie's shoulder. "That could be you, dear. Forty years of married bliss."

"Uh. Thanks. I'm happy for you. Really." She held up her cup and motioned towards the stairs.

Maybe that worked for some people. Not her. If only the Europe trip hadn't fallen through. She wouldn't have had to face him. Or heard his deep voice. Or seen his cute kid. Movie. Focus. Going to watch a movie.

Chapter Twelve

The restaurant was crowded this morning. Sophie pulled out the padded chair and threw her coat over the back before she went to the buffet counter. So far, she had enjoyed the oatmeal with raspberries and apples, the chocolate chip-orange scones, the savory cheese omelet with onions and mushrooms. Today she decided on a waffle. With a scoop of butter. And strawberries. Topped with whip cream and chocolate syrup. Now that's a breakfast that should keep her ramped up for the morning. She filled her coffee cup and walked back to her seat, taking in the dozens of white twinkle lights interwoven with fragrant greens and strung along the windowsill.

This place really knew how to make you feel cozy. She took a bite, savoring the chocolatey goodness.

"I see you haven't changed." Sam glanced at her plate.

"What?" Sophie covered her mouth with her hand.

"Waffles with all the good stuff!" He smiled.

He remembered that? It had always been her go to at cute little Coffee Corner for their Saturday morning dates.

"Daddy, I want one of those. Come on!" Darby tugged on his arm.

"Mind if we join you?"

What could she say? No? That would seem rude.

Sophie nodded.

Sam and Darby returned with plates laden with a mini waffle for Darby with all the goodies—even sprinkles on her whip cream. Sam had a large, steaming omelet, everything bagel, six slices of bacon and large coffee.

"What r we doing tu-day, Mirs Thophie?" Darby asked as she scooted up on her knees, her mouth full of waffle.

"Swallow first. She'll understand you better."

Sophie took a sip of her coffee. "Well, first we'll make some paper angels to put on the tree and I have something special to do, and last we'll practice the nativity play."

"I already know all the words to *Away in a Manger*. And all the motions. It's going to be my audition song when I try out for American Idol! Wanna hear me?"

Sam grinned.

Darby started singing, holding her arms like she held baby Jesus, eyes scrunched up in focus, shook her head, folded her hands next to her cheek. Sophie couldn't help the lump that rose in her throat. She looked at Sam and formed a heart with her fingers, motioning over her heart as if it were beating. This girl.

Darby took a big gulp of her orange juice. "That singing made my throat dry."

Sophie was sure she was going to snort milk from her nose she was laughing so hard.

They finished breakfast and bussed their dishes.

Sophie looked at Sam. "Do you want me to go ahead and take Darby?"

"Yeah, that would be great. I want to finish up the last details of the stable."

Darby grabbed Sophie's hand and they headed to the activity room.

"Miss Sophie, do you have any kids?"

"Nope. Maybe someday."

"You're not as lucky as my daddy is. He has me, and I'm the best! I tell him so *every* day and so he knows it's true." She shrugged. *Absolutely true.* She was going to miss Darby. Miss Sam. She may as well make the best of these last few days while they lasted.

The paper angels were cute. Only a few heads and wings accidentally lopped off in the process. And practice went well. She'd have to ask Megan to film it. Maybe she could use it on a resumé. If nothing else, it was sure to bring smiles and the kids would remember the story.

Sophie gathered the kids together. She whispered. "Okay, here's a secret thing we're going to do. You can't tell anyone." Their eyes grew wide. "We're going to draw names for a Secret Santa. For the next three days, you'll sneak a gift to your person and on Christmas Eve you get to find out who your person is. Sound like fun?"

Sophie had names of each family on slips of paper.

"Darby, do you want to pass the bowl around?"

Darby jumped up and down. She held the bowl, and each child took a name with a matching room number on it. Megan wrote each draw on a list.

"Miss Sophie, there's one left. This is for you." She handed her the folded paper.

She opened it slowly. Sam. And closed it quickly, pulling her lips between her teeth. How in the world did that happen?

⁂

"Do you want me to hand these boughs to you?" Justin looked up to Sam perched on top of the ladder.

"Would you? That'd be great." They had nailed slats of wood for the stable roof and were covering them with nordmann pine boughs.

"Thanks again for watching Darby last night while Sophie and I went snow shoeing."

"Not a problem. She's all Micah talks about. And Miss Sophie this and Miss Sophie that. That woman is something else." Justin glanced at Sam.

"Yup. I have to admit she's all I think about. Or want to talk about. Or talk to." *Or run my fingers through her red hair. Or set my lips to hers.*

"You're rambling, dude. You've got it bad!"

"I just don't want to ruin things like I did before. Every time I think I'm getting close, she pushes away."

"You've got to gain her trust, bro. Do something you know she liked before. Something she wouldn't expect but would warm her little heart." He handed Sam another bough. "I'm no expert. Then again, Annie and I have been married almost ten years now."

Would Sam be the one to give advice ten years from now? He certainly hoped so.

⁂

"Darby, do you want to push the cart?" Sophie had borrowed

one from the kitchen and stacked dozens of plates of decorated sugar cookies on it.

"I can do it. See how tall I'm getting? I can reach the handle just fine. I'm practically a grown-up. My daddy says I'll be driving any day now."

Sophie let out a chuckle and walked beside her, opened the glass door leading outside and onto the sidewalk. Cabins were scattered over the property, and they were making surprise deliveries to each of them.

"Okay, Darby. Knock on the door." Darby ran up to the door and rapped with her pink gloved knuckles.

"Well, hello! What do we have here?"

"We brought you cookies!" She handed a plate to the grey-haired woman. "Christmas cookies. We decorated them ourselves!"

Sophie squinched up her face. "In their activities class. Merry Christmas."

"That is a treat. Marvin? We should have brought our grandkids like we had planned."

Sophie smiled.

"Will you be here next year? I want my grandkids to join in this fun."

Probably not. But then again, miracles could happen.

They waved goodbye and walked towards the next cabin stopping to watch a squirrel scamper up a tree. A blue jay squawked at it.

"Can we give them some cookies too?"

"That would be nice to feed them, but I'm not sure all that sugar is good for them. We'll make some pinecone bird feeders tomorrow."

They continued door to door until they'd delivered all but one plate.

"Miss Sophie, can I give the last one to my dad?"

Sophie checked the time. It was way past when Sam was to have picked her up.

"Sure. Come on Darby, we've better get back!"

Sam ambled his way to the activity room, carrying a gingerbread scone and cup of peppermint mocha. Those were at least two things he knew she loved. The way to a woman's heart... Wait. That was probably diamonds or something like that.

As he got closer, he didn't hear the usual sound of kids' chatter. Huh. He peeked in the room. Lights were off. No sign of anyone. No Megan either. He searched out the window. No sign of kids or Sophie. You'd think she would have left a note. Had he forgotten about an alternate activity afterwards? He checked his phone. No texts or reminders. He called Justin.

"Hey, did you pick up Micah already?"

"Yeah, a little bit ago. Why?"

"No one is here. No sign of Darby."

"Dunno, dude. I'll let you know if I hear anything."

Sam set the scone and coffee down and went to the lobby to check the activity schedule. Nothing out of the ordinary. He went to front desk.

"Any idea where Sophie and my little girl are?"

"Not in the activity room?"

"Nope."

"Sorry, can't help you." Where the heck would they be? Sam headed to his room. Not there. He sent a text to Sophie. The exclamation point in the red circle—not delivered. Dang. Why wouldn't she have told him if she was making other plans? The woman could be rude. This was his daughter he was talking about.

He checked the restaurant. Went to Sophie's room. Finally

headed outside. She wouldn't have wandered off by herself, would she? He ran down through the trails, the loop around the cabins and finally returned to the lodge. Where could they be? What if something had happened to her? Was she hurt? Wouldn't Sophie have called? At least texted? He was beside himself. May as well wait in the lobby. They would have to pass through there to get to anywhere else.

"Daddy! I have cookies for you!" Darby barreled into him.

"Baby, where have you been? I've looked everywhere for you! I was so worried." Sam bent to her level and threw his arms around her.

"I was with Miss Sophie taking surprises to people. We brought them cookies and made them happy."

"Sam. I am so sorry. I should have let you know. We got caught up delivering cookies—"

Sam interrupted. "And you're all over my case because I didn't show up for your play practice." His look shot daggers. "This is my girl we're talking about. Don't *ever* do that again!"

"Sam!" Sophie stood there, stunned. How could he think she would ever put Darby in harm's way? "You're not the only one who cares about her. I would *never* let anything happen to her. Don't you know that by now?"

"Obviously not." Sam seethed. Thrusting Darby on his back, he stomped off.

Chapter Thirteen

"Daddy, why are you always mad at Miss Sophie? We were just doing nice things for people. You always tell me I should do nice things." Sam's felt gut punched.

Sam didn't have an answer. He wasn't always mad at Sophie, was he?

"You need to change your 'tood' and then you can marry her." Darby put her lips next to his ear and whispered. "I want her to be my mommy."

Sam felt his face flush. He took the stairs two at a time. He didn't need anyone to see him flustered. Darby slid down his back and took the key card from him to unlock the door.

As they entered the room, his phone rang.

"Hey mom. Give me a second while I help Darby off with her coat." He needed an excuse. He wasn't in the mood to talk to her or to hear about his dad.

"Okay. I'm back."

"Your dad is still in the hospital. He's not doing much better. He can talk, but he's having a hard time using his right hand. He's asking for you. When can you come see him?"

Sam started working his jaw. "Sorry, mom. We're still booked here through Christmas. I'll come the day after."

"That's three days! If you cared, you'd be here. He might not be around that long." She let out a loud sigh.

Was this another bluff? What was Sam going to say to him, anyway?

"I care. It's just that I made a commitment to Darby to be here through Christmas." *And I need a few more days to try and make things work with Sophie.*

"Okay, I see how it is. You love her more than your dad who's dying. Well, I guess I don't have anything to say to you." She hung up.

Sophie attached glistening snowflake lights to the garland scalloped along the walls. Plaid satin ribbons were hung at intervals and several large lighted balls hung from the ceiling. Someone had hung mistletoe balls at every entrance and strategically over each couch. The upcoming ball was all anyone was talking about. Community members and guests from all over attended this annual traditional event.

How had she gotten roped into decorating for the Christmas ball? Decorating would have happened whether she was there or not. She really didn't want to think about the dance. Each time she did her stomach clenched with anxiety. Truth be told, she couldn't think of anything she wanted more than to dance with Sam and be held in his arms. Flip side? That probably was not going to happen. Seemed like everything she did with Darby was wrong. That little girl was obviously his life. He didn't need Sophie to mess things up.

She sighed.

"Hey—your recruit is here. What do you need me to do?" Megan held out her hands.

"Do you know who's doing the sound system?"

"Not me, that's for sure. I think Justin has that covered."

"Good. Cuz I didn't want to be in charge of that. Cords and mics are not really my jam." She stepped off the ladder and gave the room a once over. "What are you going to wear? I didn't know about the ball till after I got here."Not entirely true. She just didn't think there would be a reason to go. And bring up old memories. Slow dances and kisses.

"I've got a couple of cute dresses. You could probably fit into one of them." Megan picked up a strand of lights. "Want to go look at them now?"

Sophie shook her head slowly.

"Come on Sophie, let's just get this out of the way. You're pretty much done here anyway."

Did she really want to look at dresses? Why did she even think she should go? Just to pine away at a guy who didn't really want her in his life?

They headed to Megan's room where she slid the closet door open. Megan pulled out three dresses and held one up.

"What's your color? You need to pick which goes best with your red hair!"

"Not pale pink, that's for sure. Three dresses? You're a regular party girl, aren't you?"

"Yeah, I just get carried away. I brought more than one so I could choose depending on what kind of mood I'm in."

Sophie fingered the soft teal chiffon and ran her fingers over the bead work on the A-line bodice.

"Try it on! You and I are about the same size."

Sophie held it up to her and looked in the mirror. She bit her bottom lip. "Go on." Megan waved her towards the bathroom.

Sophie returned, turning around so Megan could zip her up. The dress fit her perfectly. She twirled around and let the full skirt billow out around her.

"You look like a princess. Sam is going to be gaga over you! I can't wait to see how that goes down." Megan laughed.

Sophie fingered her necklace.

"Yeah. I'm not so sure I want to see how it goes down. This could really spiral."

"What's the worst that could happen?"

"I'd embarrass myself. Say something dumb. Expect him to accept me. Want to be with me."

"Sophie, I see how he looks at you. Whatever is going on in his little pea brain—you just got to be yourself. Remind him of what he loved in you before. I actually think you've already done that."

Sophie turned so Megan could unzip her dress.

"When I look at him, I have all the same feelings. Only more. Cuz now he has that adorable little girl. He's such a good dad. I wish I could be a part of that."

"He likes you. You like him. What's the problem?"

Love was more like it.

Sam adjusted the snowboard straps on Darby's feet. She was bundled up in her pink down jacket and had her thick knit hat pulled over that crazy hair, two large pompoms waving each time she turned her head. He reached in his pocket and pulled out some tinted goggles and let her put them on.

"You ready?" This wasn't her first adventure on a snowboard. Truth be told, he was pretty proud that a four-year-old could achieve this skill. But then again, she had good genes.

She gave a jump and started down the soft slope. He stood

back, hands on hips, grinning as she swerved back and forth down the slope, leaving some of the other kids in the drift. Darby reached the bottom and turned to look at Sam, pumping her fist in the air in triumph.

A mom was kneeling next to her son giving him a pep talk. She pointed at Darby, obviously letting him see that if a younger child could do it, he could too. Sam's pride meter just went up a notch. He wished Sophie was here to see it.

Maybe Darby was right. He did need an attitude adjustment. Sophie obviously cared about Darby. He was just so darned protective of his little girl. And what was keeping him from letting Sophie into their circle? Not only was she beautiful, but she was also great with kids, thoughtful, a woman of integrity. He had spent the last two years observing women. Not once did he find someone like her.

Besides, she wasn't the one who had left him. If anything, she should be the one who was cautious. The ball was in his court. He would ask if she wanted to go to the ball with him. Test the waters. Hopefully she'd say yes. If not, well, he didn't want to think about that.

Darby had climbed back up the slope and pulled on Sam's gloved hand. "Daddy, I'm gonna go again! This is so much fun. I wish Miss Sophie could watch me."

Sam only nodded.

Chapter Fourteen

"Set the manger in the middle." Sophie's left hand held her chin as she pointed with her right. "And the bales of hay can go on either side. We need them for Mary and Joseph to sit on."

Sam hoisted a bale and set it down. She let her gaze fall a little too long on his biceps.

"Sophie?" Sam looked at her. "Did you hear me?"

She gave her head a quick shake, dislodging her thoughts.

"I'm sorry. No." She bit her lip.

"What were you deep in thought about? I'm sure there are a lot of details for tonight's performance."

"It wasn't that." She held his gaze. "It was. . ."

Sam sat on one of the hay bales. "Do you feel like telling me?" Would she let him in?

"I was thinking about us." She let her eyes fall to the floor. "About before."

Sam leaned his back against the prop, gripping the front of the hay bale.

"Before I bailed on you? No pun intended." He grimaced.

She caught his gaze. "Where did things go wrong? I thought

everything was great between us. You proposed. I accepted. We set a date. I've wracked my brain for something, any little detail, that would have turned you from me." She started pacing the floor. Hesitating, she scrunched her lips into a thought before speaking

"Why did you leave me? What did I do wrong? I mean, I'm not perfect, but we had our lives planned out."

Sam heaved out a heavy breath. "You don't know how many times I've relived that moment. So many times, I stared at my phone, wanting to call you. Beg you back." He bounced his knees.

"And yet you didn't." She pressed her knuckles to her lips.

"Sophie, I was scared. I lost my job. I kept hearing my dad's voice in my head telling me what a failure I was. I didn't feel like I deserved you. Like if I stayed, I would bring you down. You had so many dreams. You deserved someone better than me."

"And look how that turned out. I'm still hoping for a teaching job. And someone to love me." Her voice was barely above a whisper. She swiped at the moisture in her eyes. "At least you have Darby."

Sam moved towards her. His heart was in his throat. He needed her to know how sorry he was. That now, looking back, and after spending these last few days together, he regretted how he handled things.

He put his hands on her shoulders. "I never meant to make you feel less than. You were everything to me." He needed to stop talking before his voice betrayed the emotion welling in him. She was still everything to him. It was all he could do to not pull her into a hug. Baby steps. Take it slow. He pulled away. He had to step back from those eyes or any restraint he had would crumble.

"Sometimes I think that in spite of how I handled things, God had a plan all along."

Sophie leaned against the wall.

"Who would have thought that I'd find joy in being a carpenter? That was thanks to Henry. And then to have been at the right place and time, as horrific as it was, to have been able to care for Darby."

"And do you think God had anything to do with us both being at this lodge at the same time?" Sophie crossed her arms. "I mean. I'm glad to see you are getting along well. You look so much more relaxed. And there's no doubt you and Darby were made for each other."

And you, Sophie, were made for me.

"Daddy?" Darby ran in and stopped. Her eyes travelled from him to Sophie. She put her hands on her hips are frowned. "What were you guys talking about, anyway?"

"Just having a little adult conversation, sweet pea. Come help us get the stage ready for your Nativity tonight." Maybe now wasn't the best time to ask Sophie to the ball.

Did that just happen? Sophie hid in the closet while she gathered the tub of costumes. How could he have a vulnerable moment, get close and then back off? That man was so exasperating! She lugged the tub out and thunked it on the ground. She removed the lid and started throwing costumes out on the stage, making sure they each had all their parts.

"Miss Sophie! I want to help."

Sophie handed Darby each piece, describing which character they went to. She pulled out the angel costume and pulled it over Darby's head, carefully easing it over her two ponytails.

"Where are my wings? I has to have wings you know."

Sophie's mouth turned up in a smile. It was hard to stay mad with that little girl around. She untied the ribbons and fastened the wings to her little body. Darby ran around in a circle, pretending to fly.

"Slow down little miss. We better take those off and go get dinner before the play." Sam carefully removed them.

"Are you set, Sophie? Okay if we leave?" Sam's eyebrows raised.

"Yeah. Sure. Thanks for your help." *And for clearing things up.* "You're bringing your guitar, right?"

Sam nodded.

Sophie finished the last details and headed to her room. She picked up her phone and called for room service. Going to the dining hall surrounded by people—certain people, wasn't where she wanted to be at the moment. Besides, she needed to collect her thoughts, try to put Sam out of her head, and make sure she was totally ready for tonight.

Sophie should feel nervous with all the hustle and bustle. Parents and family members were straggling in, expectations high. But this was her element. She loved pulling all the pieces together—the practice, the costumes, the set. The proud moment when it all came together.

She breathed out a little prayer. *For your glory. . .*

Megan helped coral all the kids behind the scenes, making sure all their costumes were straight, dabbing on bits of rouge and lip gloss.

Okay. Sophie let out a breath and smiled at them, giving a thumbs up.

"Welcome everyone. First, I'd like to thank all of you for entrusting your children to me this week. I think I've learned as much from them as they've learned from me."

Someone in the audience let out a whoop. She smiled.

"And now, let's begin." She lowered the lights and beckoned Bradley, a middle schooler to the stage.

"Caesar Augustus told everyone they had to be counted. And so, everybody had to travel to the town they were born in."

Joseph led Mary who waddled in trying to hold the pillow under her gown.

"Come along Mary. We'll be in Bethlehem soon."

As they walked down the center aisle, Joseph pretended to knock on doors.

"Can anybody let us stay here? My wife is gonna have a baby."

They came to the stable where those dressed as cows and sheep stood, convincingly mooing and baaing. The audience laughed. Mary hid behind the set and dropped the pillow and returned.

"And Mary gave birth to a boy, and she wrapped him in a blanket and laid him in a manger."

"Shepherds were watching their sheep in the fields."

Several sheep started bleating as two shepherds shooed them with their crooks.

"And suddenly there shone a bright light."

Darby ran out before them, catching her halo as it tilted. "Hey! Look up! See that star shining? My dad made that for Miss Sophie."

How could Sophie have missed the beautifully hand carved star at the peak of the stable? A light shone through it, casting beams.

"Dudes, it's Jesus! Come on. You gotta see him!"

Darby waved them to the stable. The audience erupted in laughter.

Sam sat on a stool in front of them and strummed chords. The familiar words of *Away in a Manger* filled the air. Parents joined in as they watched their children do hand motions to the words.

Sophie looked at Sam. His easy, gentle way with the guitar. His deep voice leading the words. She felt her heart slowly shift. She wanted to be angry, but any bitterness evaporated when she looked at him. This. Joining together on a common goal. She wanted this forever.

Chapter Fifteen

S am turned on the radio and adjusted the wipers to intermittent. Interrupting his last few days at the lodge with Sophie was not what he had in mind. His hands tightened on the steering wheel. That man was bound and determined to interfere with his life clear to the end.

"You okay?" Sophie touched his arm.

Sam shrugged. "You've got frown lines and look like you want to punch something." Sophie let out a soft laugh.

Sam side-eyed her. Let out a sigh.

"I don't know how to get out from under my dad's control. Or my mom's either, for that matter. Believe me, I've tried to understand them. But clearly, that's never going to happen."

"You're their only child now. I'm sure your mom just wants you to make peace with your dad before he dies."

"Did he have to pick this week?" He slammed his palm onto the steering wheel. "I'm not staying at the hospital a minute longer than I have to. She asked me to come. I'm coming. But I'm not making any promises."

Sophie glanced in the back seat at the sleeping Darby. "Let's take Darby in long enough to say hello and I'll take her for a walk to the cafeteria for a treat."

Sam nodded. Sophie had been there when his mom had called, begging him to come see his dad, saying he wasn't going to last much longer. He expected to get there and find out this was another one of their manipulative moves. But what if he was wrong?

He was grateful Sophie had offered to come along. She had a calming effect on him. He still hadn't asked her to the ball. Maybe now would be a good time. As he started to open his mouth, a driver cut him off. An expletive escaped from his mouth. No, now wasn't the time.

Sophie's phone buzzed. She read the text and squealed. "It's the international school. They offered me a job!" Her jaw dropped as she turned to look at him.

"That's. . ." Sam ran his hand through his beard. "Nice. You've been hoping for that." He swallowed. So much for hoping things were heading in the right direction.

She put her phone in her lap. "They want me to start the second week of January. The position is just till June. But if things go well, they'll keep me on for the following year."

That was only a week away. "I'm happy for you, Sophie. I really am." Did his voice reflect the lie?

Okay Lord, is this you saying we should take a longer break?

Sam pulled into the parking lot and turned off the car. He whooshed out a long breath.

"Ready?" Sophie opened the back door and helped Darby out of her car seat.

Sam's feet felt like lead, one step in front of the other until they found room 205. The only light in the room filtered in through the window. A monitor beeped, little blips modulating on the screen. His dad looked small under the sheet—his face wan with the left side of his jaw slack.

"You made it." His mom put down a crossword puzzle and rose from her chair. Even here in the hospital where no one could possibly care, her face was made up and she looked like she had just come from the beauty shop.

"Grandma!" Darby ran into her arms and glanced at his dad. "What's wrong with grandpa?"

His mom smoothed Darby's bangs from her eyes. "He's not feeling well, baby."

"Is that my girl?" His dad adjusted himself in the bed. "Come give me a hug." He reached out his arms, the tube dangling from his stronger hand. Darby gave a tentative hug and backed away.

"Come on Darby, let's go see if we can find a snack. You're probably hungry after that long drive." She hopped down and took Sophie's hand. Sophie gave a slight nod to Sam. He didn't blame her for not wanting to enter any kind of conversation with them.

"How are you feeling, dad?" It surprised Sam how flat his voice sounded.

"How the h— do you think I'm feeling? Look at me! You've got eyes, don't you?"

"I'm sure it's frustrating for you to be here."

His dad nodded. "Was that Sophie? I thought you two weren't together anymore."

Sam cleared his throat. "We're not, exactly."

"What's that supposed to mean? She was the best thing that ever happened to you, except maybe Darby."

Sam huffed. "Everything is a war with you." He turned to the window.

"That's cuz life *is* a war. Illness comes? You have to fight it. Kids make bad decisions? It becomes a battle. Listen to me. I may not have long to live, but if I've learned one thing— the things you love are worth fighting for." Sam turned back.

His dad swiped the back of his hand against the drool on his lips.

"You didn't fight for Sophie. You let your rejection come in the way of your relationship. And as usual, you took the coward's way out." He shook his head. "Real men stay and fight. Even when it's tough. They fight for the things they love." He fell back against his pillow.

"And is that why we're always fighting? Because if it is, that's a weird way of showing you love me."

His dad motioned for a glass of water. Sam handed it to him. "I'm sorry son. It's the only way I know how."

"Sam," his mom's face was pained, "your dad needs to rest."

"I'll see myself out." Sam leaned down and gave her a peck on her cheek.

"He means well, son." *Yeah, I'm sure he does.*

⁂

They had ridden home in silence. Sam needed to process. She needed to process. What was taking the job in Germany going to say? That it was more important than Sam? She wasn't even sure where they stood. If she were honest, she wasn't sure which she could give up—Germany which was a sure thing? Or Sam.

He hadn't asked her to the ball. Maybe he was worried they'd get too close. She wouldn't blame him. He had Darby to think of. She should give back Megan's dress. And go ahead and take the job.

They pulled up to the lodge.

"Sam, thank you for whittling the star for the stable. It was beautiful." He shrugged.

"I have something for you, too. Um, Darby chose me for your secret Santa." She reached into her bag and retrieved a package.

He pulled it out of the wrapping and looked at her. "When did you take this?"

"The other day when you guys were sledding. You were so cute." She smiled. "Darby made the frame."

"That might be the best present I've ever received. Thank you." He reached over and squeezed her hand. She nodded and slid out of the truck. Now was not the time to get mushy.

Chapter Sixteen

"Come on, daddy. We're 'sposed to watch the Nutcracker. With real ballet dancers. Hurry! Miss Sophie doesn't want us to be late." Darby yanked on his hand.

Sam watched Sophie greeting each child, getting down to their eye level. That smile. The smiles she brought to others. In this one thing, his dad was right. He'd do whatever it took to look at that smile every single day.

"Hey man, could you give me a hand today?" Justin approached Sam, Micah's hand in his. "I need help setting up the ball for tonight."

"Sure. Of course." The ball. Sam swallowed. Now probably wasn't the best time to ask Sophie. He could wait until he picked Darby up after activities. Or chicken out altogether like he'd done on the way home from the hospital. His hands were starting to sweat just thinking about it. Besides, she was just going to leave for Europe. Why hope?

Sam followed Justin to the ballroom. Decorations were already hung—swags of garland, glitter balls hanging from the ceiling. Mistletoe. Yeah, about that. The memory flooded in—

kissing her the night he had proposed. Soft lips. His hands in her red hair.

"Dude! You okay? You look like you're frozen."

Pink stained Sam's angled cheeks. Justin laughed and slapped Sam on the back.

"Uh, yeah." He rubbed the back of his neck.

"Give me a hand here with the sound system." Justin handed Sam a cable and a mic.

"Can you attach it to the mic? I'll hook up the other end. Any requests for songs on the karaoke playlist?"

Sam's eyes scanned the room. The decorations. There was no hesitation—his mind travel back to a memory he hadn't visited in so long it resembled a dream—frequent karaoke nights with Sophie. And that one song in particular. . .

This might be the only chance he had left.

Sam took measured steps down the hall to the activity room. He should tell Darby to relay the message that he wants her to go with him to the ball. Nahh. That would be pretty chicken, even though he knew Darby would jump up and down at the opportunity. He stopped and leaned against the wall and adjusted his beanie. What was wrong with him? He was a grown man for pity's sake. It was just a dance.

But no, it was more than a dance. It was a chance to redeem himself. To tell her he loved her. To let her know he never wanted anything to come between them again.

But what about the international job? How would that work?

Darby flung open the door and came running to him, nearly knocking him down with her exuberant hug. "Did you have fun today with Miss Sophie?"

"Yeah, we made pretty glass ornaments!"

"I can't wait to see yours."

"Come on." She grabbed his hand and started pulling him to the door. "They're in the room."

Sam entered the room and looked around for Sophie. The room was dark, the lights turned off. So much for asking her out.

"Here's my ornament. Miss Sophie said you need to take it for me. It's very fragile."

"Where is Miss Sophie, anyway?"

Darby shrugged and handed him the ornament, glittery fingernail polish adorning her little fingers. "Can we put it on the big tree in the lounge?"

"Sure baby." Sam breathed out his anxiety.

Darby skipped over to the tree, the lights twinkling and shining against the silver stars and other ornaments. As Darby pulled the ornament out of the bag, it slid from her fingers and crashed onto the tile floor.

"No!" A loud wail pierced the air. "Miss Sophie said I was s'post to be careful." Big tears ran down her rosy cheeks.

Sam knelt to her level, placed his large hands on her shoulders and looked her in the eye. "Listen, it was pretty. And you did a really nice job on it. But sometimes just making things is what's fun."

"You don't understand, daddy. If I'm not good, Santa isn't going to bring me any presents." She let out a big hiccuping sob. Sam patted her on the back.

"Come on. We'll get some paper and write him a letter. You can explain. I'm sure he'll be okay with that." He wiped her tears with his thumb.

Sam got a piece of paper and envelope from the check-in clerk and handed it to Darby. "Let's get some cocoa and you can write your letter up in our room."

Sam soon got her settled with a pen and some colored pencils. She snuggled Chester on her lap, asking him how to spell Santa and saying each letter as she tried to sound it out.

Sam needed to shower before he got dressed up. He let the hot water run down his head and back, washing away the tension. He'd blown asking Sophie. Maybe he should just skip asking her. See if she showed up on her own. Then ask her to dance. Tell her he loved her. Sweep her off her feet. . .

He toweled off and pulled on his slacks. "All done with your letter?"

"Yeah. I hope I wrote everything right." Sam read it.

> Dear Santa
> I m sory I brok the ornment. I hop ur not mad.
> Cuz daddy needs to get Sophie for Christmas
> Luv Darby

Sam swallowed. Hard. He couldn't let this little girl down.

"Go get your pretty dress so you can be ready for the ball. Then we'll mail your letter. I saw a Santa mailbox out by the reindeer coral."

"Can Chester come too? He's never been to a dance before."

"I don't see why not." Sam smiled. He put on a white button-down shirt and wrestled with his tie. Suits and ties were not in his comfort zone. But a guy's gotta do whatever it takes. A jolt of anxiety hit his stomach wondering if Sophie would even show up.

"Okay doll. Let me run a brush through your hair and let's go." Darby handed him a barrette with a ribbon attached. He took hold of her hand. "Who put nail polish on you?"

"Miss Sophie. She said I should look pretty for the dance."

"Well, you look gorgeous."

"You look gorgeous too." She took his hand and hugged Chester to her chest.

As they walked down the hall, the mixed aromas of barbecued chicken, pastas and baked potatoes wafted towards them.

"I'm hungry. Can we eat first?"

"Uh. Sure. Yeah. We better do that." What kind of dad doesn't remember to feed his daughter dinner?

Sam filled her plate with macaroni and cheese, the sauce creamy and gooey. "Be careful with it. You don't want to ruin your pretty dress."

He looked around the dining hall. No sign of Sophie. His nerves tingled through him. He wanted to see her. Ask her if she was going. Then again, he didn't want to see her. What if he was dressed up and she said she wasn't? It would be all for nothing.

Sam gave Darby a napkin to wipe her mouth and they bussed their dishes.

The reindeer were smaller than he remembered them. Their doe eyes occasionally looked at Sam and Darby between grazing. Their antlers were like velvet. Darby began to climb the fence.

Sam lifted her down. "Don't want to ruin your princess dress, doo. Let's go mail your letter. I can hear the music starting to play."

Sam gave Darby the letter and lifted her as she slid it through the opening.

"There." She brushed her hands together. Being a dad had

huge responsibilities. Was he right in letting her believe that Santa would grant her wish? That somehow her mistakes could keep her from her dreams?

"I has to go to the bathroom." Sam took her to the guest ladies' room and waited outside, hoping to get a glimpse of a red headed beauty. Maybe he should text Sophie and see if she's coming. He pulled out his phone and stared at it. Then returned it to his pocket.

Darby shoved the door open. Her eyebrows were pulled into a frown. "I can't find Chester."

"Did you leave him in the bathroom?"

"No, he's not there."

"Did you even bring him?"

"Yes. Of course, I brought him. What do you think, daddy?"

"Maybe you left him at dinner. Let's go check there." They retraced their steps, but the little raccoon wasn't there.

"Let's just go to the dance and we can look for him later." Darby pulled away, put her hands on her hips and scowled.

"I can't just leave him somewhere. He'll be lonely. We has to find him now!" Sam whooshed a sigh.

"Okay." Sam drew out the word and placed his palm on his forehead. Where else should they look?

They trudged back outside. He stopped by the mailbox and looked around. No sign of a little raccoon. They retraced their steps to the reindeer. Nothing.

Tears trickled down her face. Sam picked her up and hugged her, certain drool and snot would be rubbed into his jacket.

He carried her inside, sat down on the bench in the lobby and held her.

Chapter Seventeen

Sophie screwed the cap back on the sparkly nail polish. Polishing Darby's nails somehow made her heart glow. It was such a simple act. But doing nails? That was something moms do with their daughters. And Darby was sadly lacking that in her life. Not that Sam wasn't an excellent dad. There was no doubt in her mind that he was. Just watching the way he looked at her. If it was a cartoon there'd be little hearts flying in the air around him. She smiled.

Darby had been so excited about going to the ball. Sophie wished she could be that excited. More than anything, she wanted to be back in Sam's arms.

She pulled the gown out of the closet and hung it on the door.

Her phone buzzed. "Hey, Claire! I was just thinking about you."

"I know. Because you're always thinking about me. How was your day?"

"Fine. I was just trying to make up my mind about whether to go to the Winter Ball or not."

"Did you bring a dress?"

"No, but Megan had several and lent me one. It's beautiful. And it fits. It's just—"

"You worried about Sam? Did he ask you to go with him?"

"No." Sophie's shoulders dropped. She put her phone on speaker and began to brush her hair.

"Did you ask him? It's the twentieth century you know."

"I know. I was going to text him."

"But you didn't." Sophie leaned her head to the side and pulled the brush through her the length of her hair.

"Okay. Here's what you're going to do. You're going to fluff up those curls, pull some back— braid a little bit of it and put a barrette in it. It wouldn't hurt to put a little makeup on. A touch of lip gloss. Wiggle yourself into that dress. Then Facetime so I can see it."

After a few contortions, Sophie managed to pull up the zipper. She fixed her hair like Claire had suggested and dabbed a bit of gloss on her lips. She fingered her necklace. Then she Facetimed her sister.

"Oh. My. Gosh. There is no way he's not going to sweep you in his arms and carry you away. He should never have let you go to begin with. The jerk."

"No, he shouldn't have."

Claire waved her hand like she was fanning herself. She laughed. "Shoulders back. Turn your head and. . ." They both ptooey'd at the same time. Sophie bent over in a fit of giggles.

"Let me know how it goes. I'll be praying for you."

Sophie blew her a kiss and pushed end. She should have told her she got the job. She'd tell her next time.

She made her way down the hall. The music was playing, and laughter billowed from the hall. She stood in the doorway, willing the butterflies to cease. The house lights were low, but the outdoor string lights draped across the ceiling, adding twinkle to the glittery snowflakes hanging from the ceiling.

Justin sat on a small stage manning the DJ equipment. His eyebrows raised when he caught her eye. He sported a huge encouraging grin.

She scanned the room, but there was no sign of Sam. Or Darby. Well, she'd mingle with the others. Megan crossed the room to her, a handsome hunk holding her hand.

"Who is this beauty? Megan, you didn't tell me you had a gorgeous friend!"

Megan shoved her shoulder into his. "Sophie, this is Mark." Megan looked her over.

"That dress really works for you."

Sophie smiled and held out her hand. "Hello Mark."

"Did you come alone? I could probably find you a perfect guy." He winked.

"I'm good. But thanks." *I already have the perfect guy. I think. Maybe.* She glanced around. Again.

Couples of all ages were dancing, smiles on their faces. Mark guided Megan to the floor and pulled some swing dance moves. Sophie couldn't help but smile at their smooth moves. She and Sam had perfected some of the same. Where was he, anyway?

"Miss Sophie! Wanna dance?" Micah looked up at her with his deep brown eyes. "You look pretty. Like a princess!"

"Hey Micah. I'd love to. You look pretty good yourself. I love your tie." Sophie held her hand out to him. Justin had cued up *Rockin' around the Christmas Tree* and Sophie laughed as Micah moved to the beat. Not bad for a five-year-old. Well, if Sam wasn't going to show up, she could enjoy this little date.

Who was she kidding? She'd be gone in a few days and all this week would be a thing of the past. She'd get on with her life and try to forget he ever existed.

"Okay friends and family. It's time to switch to some karaoke. Just come on over and put your name on the list." *What the heck. I may as well.* Sophie and Sam had sung together on their first date. After that, it had become a regular thing—his deep voice blending with her soprano. If only he were here.

"Darby, is this yours?" Megan had just come out of the women's room. "It was behind the door."

"Chester! You found him!" Darby jumped off Sam's lap and ran to her, grabbed her raccoon, and wrapped her arms tightly around him. Sam let out a relieved breath and relaxed his shoulders.

"You'd think it was the end of the world—losing a stuffed toy. That little girl had a pretty epic meltdown." Sam shrugged.

"Dad life." Megan laughed. "Here," she pulled out a tissue. "You could use a little sprucing up before you head into that ballroom to your big girl." She winked.

"Daddy, come on. I hear Miss Sophie singing."

Sam looked towards the ballroom.

My heart is broken
My dreams are gone

Sam stepped up to the mic beside her, joining his rich voice to hers.

You were the one

Who created my song

Sam gazed at her, glad that she sang the next phrase. He wasn't sure he could get past the lump in his throat to continue.

Sophie kept her eyes focused on the back wall, harmonizing, blending her voice with his. She touched her throat, her fingers grazing the sapphire necklace dangling there. Sam took her hand, wanting to wipe her tears that threatened to spill over.

If there was a way
I could relive that day

I'd turn night into light
Bring back what's right

And I'd walk through the storm
I'd swim every sea
Whatever it takes
I will relive that day

Every eye turned towards them. Seconds of silence ticked by, and the place exploded with applause and cheers. Darby ran up and grabbed each of their hands. She pulled them to the hanging mistletoe.

"Kiss her! Kiss her! Kiss her!" The crowd started clapping to the beat of her chant.

Sam bent towards her, glanced at her lips, hesitated, touched his lips to hers. There was no turning back.

Chapter Eighteen

Sophie threw her remaining clothes into her suitcase. She was glad for the week's paycheck which would cover the cost of her fare to Germany. She hoped she was making the right decision. Sam showing up to the ball and singing with her? That was magical. His lips on hers? She sighed. She wanted that forever. But she just wasn't sure she could trust him to stay.

She rolled her suitcase to the lobby.

"Daddy, you need to help her. She can't lift that heavy thing by herself."

Sophie looked at Sam. Her heart ached but she braved a smile. She let her hair fall to cover her face. He didn't need to see how torn she was, see the tears struggling to break free.

"May I?"

Sophie swallowed and nodded as he hoisted it into the back of her car.

"You'll let me know when you get there?"

"Yeah. Of course. I'll message you."

Sam walked her to the driver's side and opened the door.

"Thank you, Sam. For everything." He leaned to give her a

kiss. She turned her head so his lips grazed her cheek, then started the car. She needed to get out of here before she changed her mind.

※

Justin put his arm around Sam's shoulders as they watched her car roll away.

"Dude, you okay?"

"Negative." His throat went dry. He ran his hand over his face.

"When's her flight?"

"Tomorrow." He glanced at Darby and Micah chasing each other around the lounge.

"And you're just going to let her go? What's to keep you here, man? I mean, Darby's not in school yet. You can be a carpenter anywhere."

What was to keep me here? My dad? Nope. I'm not going to let him be the deciding factor. Besides, wasn't he the one that said I should go after her? Maybe this time my dad is right.

"Darby, come on. We've got to get packed up. Places to go. Things to do. People to see."

※

Sam hopped out of the Lyft and helped Darby wiggle into her Paw Patrol backpack. He quickly unzipped the top to be sure Chester was safely inside. No sense repeating the chaos of the other night.

The driver unloaded their bags and Sam gave a quick salute.

"Let's hurry, doo." He grabbed her hand. "We've got to catch Miss Sophie."

Sophie adjusted her backpack, replacing it from the security check. She took a few steps towards her gate and turned at the sound of a giggle. There, in front of her stood Sam and Darby holding signs. Sophie turned her head upside down in order to read Darby's. The little girl quickly adjusted her sign.

Pic us!
My dad will carve for schnitzel

A colored picture of a raccoon eating a schnitzel grinned at her. Sam held one that said:

Ich bin bis über beide Ohren verliebt

Sophie gave a quizzical look. Her German wasn't exactly the best. Sam grinned and turned it over.

"I'm in love over both ears!"

A bubble of laughter escaped her lips. A wide smile spread over Sam's bearded face. They threw down their signs and ran to her for a group hug.

"Miss Sophie, we're going with you. Daddy says he couldn't let you go."

Sam placed his hand on Darby's head. "She's right. The question is, do you want me to re-propose to you here? Or wait for an idyllic spot in Germany?"

Sophie threw her arms around his neck and kissed him like never before. He wasn't the same man he had been three years before. The man before her was willing to put aside all his fears and insecurities and lay down his life for her.

And this time, she wanted to be the one to propose. To hear that one enduring word—

Yes.

Afterword

You may enjoy listening to the audio version.
It includes the music and the song.

$$\mathcal{N}uns\ with\ \mathcal{G}uns$$

A holiday caper

An encounter ensues when a man wearing bunny slippers steals the van from the Sisters of Mercy, thrusting them into pandemonium with a group of ex-cons.

Chapter 1

The only thought invading his head the week Bernardo was released from his two-year stint in the clink, was to see his daughter Amelia. She had been three when he was convicted of stealing an assault rifle from an FBI car. He remembered those irresistible dimples he liked to kiss, and the smell of her soft curly brown hair that he combed after her bath.

His wife wasn't too happy about his jail time and didn't come to visit him or let him see their daughter. Not that he blamed her. Marie hadn't met him outside when he was released, and he wasn't looking forward to seeing her reaction to him showing up at their door. Maybe he'd be able to convince her that he'd changed. And he had, hadn't he? He had gone through counseling and was going to start fresh. Get a job. A real job with a real paycheck. Be able to support Marie and their daughter. He could do this. She was a good woman and deserved his best.

He knocked on the door and was surprised to hear little footsteps and then laid eyes on his daughter. She stopped still and looked up at him, expressionless. Her deep dark chocolate eyes stared at him; her curly hair pulled into a long pony. She looked just like her mama. Marie came up behind her, wrapped her arm protectively around Amelia's waist and pulled her in.

"What are *you* doing here?" Marie's eyes narrowed.

"I'm out. I wanted to see you and Amelia."

Marie rolled her deep brown eyes, the same ones he used to gaze into before...

"Two excruciating years without a word and now you want to waltz in here and disrupt our lives? I don't think that's a good idea." She released Amelia. "Go sit on the couch and finish watching your show, baby."

"I just want to talk to you. I don't expect you to welcome me, but could you just hear me out?"

Marie reluctantly moved aside and motioned her head to the kitchen table. The room was spotless. Dishes were put away and the table was wiped. The floor was swept, and the shine reflected the overhead light.

"You never came to visit me." Bernardo's shoulders slumped.

"I thought it would be better for Amelia not to see the inside of a jail."

"But *you* could have come."

She shook her head. She set the kettle on the stove and turned up the gas.

"Listen, I'm sorry. What I did was really stupid. But that was two years ago. I've changed. I'm not the same man."

"And how am I supposed to know that? You're gonna have to build some trust here, you know."

"I know." He started to reach for her hand, and she pulled it away.

"Tell me about Amelia. Is she in school?"

"Yeah. Kindergarten."

"Does she like her teacher? Does she have friends?"

"She does." The tea kettle whistled, and she shut off the gas. "Tea?"

"Sure."

"You still like that licorice flavor?" She opened a drawer with several boxes in it.

"You remember that?" He watched her pour the water over the bag and hand him the cup, the one that said *I love my dad*. His eyes grew misty.

"Babe, I'd do anything to repair the damage I've caused. Leaving you a single mom and not helping with the bills." He lowered his head.

She set the tea before him. He wrapped his hands around the mug and let the fragrant steam warm his face. He wished the steam could melt the ice between them.

"Bernardo, there's something you need to know. Amelia has a medical condition. The doctors performed extensive tests. She needs expensive medication that I can't afford, and state health insurance isn't going to cover it." A tear slipped down her cheek. "She's gonna die, Bernardo."

That had been two weeks ago. Marie had allowed him to spend some time with Amelia. He'd spent a day with her at school, took her for ice cream, and a movie—not all on one day. She wore out easily. Marie hadn't been ready to let him move back in, so he'd resorted to couch hopping. Not ideal, but better than living in his jeep, or worse yet, sleeping on the sidewalk.

Joey Lagratto swiped a hand down his tattooed face, his eyes closed, and let it rest there as he whooshed a long breath. Getting caught was one of the risks of pulling a heist. He just had to figure out the next step. He reached for his phone and tapped in a few numbers.

"Bernardo, I need you to take care of an item for me while we're out of commission. Meet me at four."

"What's in it for me?"

"Don't worry, you'll get your fair share." Bernardo's shoulders tensed. He didn't like being in a position to let Joey get the upper hand. But for now, he felt like he had no choice. He'd been couch surfing at his house more than anywhere else along with the five others who had been in jail with Joey. There was always a price to pay.

Bernardo nervously tossed a Rubik's cube up and down. He slid into his navy green jeep, the paint faded and worn through to the base and coughed the engine to life, leaving a trail of exhaust fumes in its wake. Weaving between cars on the D.C. highway, he thought of how his reward would be enough to get him on his feet. No more couch hopping. Or digging in the garbage cans for his next meal. His hands tightened on the steering wheel.

A glance at the mirror showed someone tailing him. He tested it out, turning at the next exit and into an old neighborhood, swerving into the left lane, and passing a semi-truck. No doubt about it—he was being pursued.

Bernardo parked the jeep in a one-way alley and jumped out. He slid the Rubik's cube into his sweatshirt pocket and exited the other side. He walked nonchalantly along the sidewalk wearing the bunny slippers he had run out of the house with. He slid a glance back. No one was going to keep him from this job. It had to end in success. He had to save his daughter.

About the Author

Jan Johnson has been writing since fourth grade when she wrote and her dad published The Little Red Man, a space story. That was back in the day when we were all sure aliens lived on Mars.

Jan lives on a sheep farm in Brownsmead, Oregon a mile from the Columbia River with her husband Ed. Don't mistake living on a farm as meaning she likes animals. Well, she actually does—from a distance.

She's passionate about building relationships, meeting new people and hearing their stories. You know what they say—Love God, Love People.

When she isn't writing, starting something new, or podcasting, she catches up with her ten children who are scattered hither and yon.

Connect with her at jan-johnson.com where you'll find links to her books and can listen to both podcasts—Women of the Northwest and Just Talkin' About Jesus

Amazon for all books

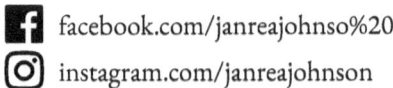

facebook.com/janreajohnso%20

instagram.com/janreajohnson